"Kacie? What is that?" My teacher's massive body loomed over me. "May I have it, please?" She held out a thick hand.

I squeezed my eyes shut and handed the paper over. You've never seen such a major fit. She paraded me to the door in front of everyone. From behind, I heard the whole class jeering, "Ooh, Kacie. Busted." I could have died.

Risky Friends

by Julie Anne Peters

Willowisp
Press®

To All My Family,
All My Love

Published by Willowisp Press
801 94th Avenue North, St. Petersburg, Florida 33702

Copyright © 1993 by Willowisp Press,
a division of PAGES, Inc.

Printed in the United States of America

2 4 6 8 10 9 7 5 3 1

ISBN 0-87406-646-8

One

I overslept by twenty minutes. Then I somehow shorted out my blow dryer, split the only fingernail I had ever managed to grow longer than a nub, and poured an entire glass of grape juice down the front of my new white silk blouse. By the time I slid into algebra class, losing my race with the late bell and breaking the strap on my sandals, I suspected this was going to be a record-breaking rotten day.

"Clear your desks, everyone. It's time for a pop quiz," Mrs. Tannenbaum said. The collective moan seemed to echo off the Colorado foothills.

Our algebra teacher was built like a Christmas tree, with a little pointy head and spreading hips. Her first name was Olive. We couldn't resist giving her a nickname: "Oh Tannenbaum."

"Quiet, please," she snapped, passing out the tests.

My pencil broke. I sighed, scribbled "Kacie Shannon" with a felt-tipped marker across the top of the page, and began. To my amazement, I could actually work most of the problems. That was probably only because my best friend, Vicky Anselli, is a whiz with anything having to do with numbers, and she had helped me with my algebra homework.

"Oh, no," moaned Skye Collinsworth, this girl who sat across the aisle. "I can't do these. I don't know how to do even one of them. I feel sick." She turned her pale face toward me.

Was she serious? About the sick part, I mean. It would be just my luck to have someone lose breakfast in front of me today. I was about to ask if she was okay when Oh Tannenbaum twisted her trunk to scowl in our direction. I quickly lowered my eyes, pretending to concentrate.

Skye's hand shot up high in the air.

"Mrs. Tannenbaum?"

"Yes, Skye?"

"May I please go to the restroom?"

Oh Tannenbaum's eyes narrowed. "After the quiz," she said.

Skye pleaded, "But I have to go *now*. I really do."

"Then hand in your paper."

Skye slumped over her desk instead, exhaling noisily. I made a sympathetic noise. Can you believe some teachers?

Oh Tannenbaum shuffled to the other side of the classroom to answer a question. When I glanced sideways at Skye, I noticed a tear plop onto her quiz.

"If I flunk this class my father will be furious," she whispered to me. "I'm already grounded for a *C-* I got on my English paper last week. I was up all night studying for a history test, and I just didn't have time for algebra."

She rested her cheek on her crossed arms, eyes brimming with tears. We'd never actually spoken before, just smiled at each other once or twice since school had started a month earlier. But I understood Skye's problem. If Vicky didn't help me with homework, I'd never be able to keep up. Middle school was tough, and so far eighth grade was no exception.

I couldn't believe Skye's father actually grounded her for a *C-*. *D* maybe, but *C*? *C* is average, right? What's wrong with being average?

Skye buried her head in her arms and began to cry steadily. And then, a second later, a loud, heart-wrenching sob suddenly escaped. I couldn't stand it. Oh Tannenbaum was deliberately ignoring her. She waddled out of the classroom to chitchat with another teacher in the hall.

And in that single moment, of a single day, in a single year, I made the biggest mistake of my life. I passed my test to Skye.

She raised her head in slow motion, sniffed and wiped her eyes. Then, flashing me a grateful smile, she quickly copied the answers onto her test.

After class Skye caught up with me in the hall. "Gosh, Kacie. You really saved my life, you know." She smiled warmly. "Why did you do it, anyway? I mean, we're not even friends."

I shrugged. "Call it temporary insanity.

Just don't tell anyone, okay?"

"I wouldn't breathe a word," she said covering her heart. "What do you think I am—a Candace Torrey?"

I burst out laughing. Candace Torrey's reputation as the mouth of Mountain View Middle School was obviously widespread. Last week she'd started a rumor that Cameron Griff was sneaking over to Tara McClure's house every night. The truth was that their parents got married over the summer, which made them stepbrother and stepsister. They lived together!

Skye said, "I haven't ever actually introduced myself, have I? I mean, you probably don't even know my last name!"

"Collinsworth, right?" I asked.

Skye looked surprised.

"Small town," I explained. "You were here at the end of last year, weren't you?"

Nodding, Skye said, "I started at the end of April. My father and I moved here right after—"

She stopped short and looked away.

After what? I wondered. Obviously, Skye didn't want to talk about it, so I changed the subject. "Do you like living in Lafayette?" I asked. "I know it's kind of a small-time place, but the people here are really nice."

"So far it's okay. At least it's not totally removed from civilization. I mean, the Boulder Mall is only a few miles away, right?" Skye smiled teasingly.

"Hey, don't forget. We have our very own McDonald's now, too."

"Ooh, sub-urban," she said, and we both cracked up.

While I paused at my locker to unload/reload for my next class, Skye leaned against the locker next to mine. "I don't know about the people here, though." She sighed. "I've had a hard time making friends." But then she suddenly brightened and elbowed me as the entire football team sprinted down the hall in gym shorts. "On the other hand, the guys are awesome."

My eyes followed hers. At the exact same moment, we both let out our breath in a dreamy sigh, then sputtered into giggles.

I spun the combination lock and yanked my bent, stuck locker door open. Like an unleashed tornado, books crashed and papers swirled out into the hall. Skye scrambled around to help me retrieve everything.

"Thanks," I said. "Where's your next class?"

Skye tossed her long blond hair over one shoulder. "It's clear over in the annex." She made a face. "I have history there, with 'Fish- lips' Fuller. Glub, glub."

I rolled my eyes in sympathy. Just then the warning bell rang. I slammed my locker shut, snapped the lock on it and hustled down the hall toward French class. Over my shoulder I hollered, "You'd better hurry, Skye. You're going to be late."

She caught up with me. "That's okay," she said. "If I miss anything, you know what they say: history always repeats itself."

I laughed.

Skye added, "I'll walk with you. I really do owe you, Kacie. You don't know how much I appreciate what you did."

"Forget it, Skye," I answered. "You don't owe me anything. Really."

Two

"I thought you were going to wear your new silk blouse today," Vicky said. I was sprawled across her bed after school, mesmerized by the fluorescent lavender polish she was carefully applying to her toenails.

"You know, I've been looking at that blouse," I replied. "It's definitely the wrong color. It doesn't go with very much."

From her desk chair Vicky gave me a sideways glance. "White doesn't go with much? Come on. What did you do? Spill something on it?"

I rolled onto my back and fluffed a pillow under my neck. Upside down, I saw her tilt her head toward me. I stared at the ceiling.

"Okay, so I did. Grape juice."

"You're kidding! Kace, what am I going to do with you?" She flung a pom-pom at my head.

That hurt. Not physically, but it was a painful reminder that she'd made the cheerleading squad and I hadn't. Vicky didn't mean it that way, though. She didn't have a mean bone in her body.

"What you can do is find me a date for the Harvest Dance," I answered, only half-joking. "Who did you decide to go with, anyway?"

"Actually, I haven't decided," Vicky said, pursing her lips. "John Masius asked me first, so I guess I should say yes. But Phil Ronkowski is so sweet that I'd really rather go with him. Then, get this: this morning, Kyle Zimmer asked me."

I bolted upright. "Kyle Zimmer? Are you serious? Class president?"

Vicky sighed dreamily and nodded. "He's pretty cute. Those big brown eyes remind me of that puppy I had in kindergarten. Remember Potato?"

"The dog who piddled his way to the pound?"

Vicky wrinkled her nose. "Get serious, Kace. What should I do? Who would you go with?"

"Any of your rejects, okay?" I scootched to the foot of the bed to watch as she initialed her big toenail with a calligraphy pen—curly *V*, curly *A*.

"What's the matter?" asked Vicky. Her thick, black braid swung gently when she turned her face toward me. "Rob's taking you, isn't he?"

"Yeah, but I'm tired of always going with Rob. It's like dating my brother. We've been friends a long time and I like Rob. I really do. But that's all it is—friendship. I thought this year would be different. You know, our last year of middle school? Just once I'd like to go on a real live date. With someone totally great—like Daniel Oakes." I grabbed a pillow and hugged it to my chest.

Vicky shook her head. "You've had a major crush on him for two years now. Why don't you just call him up and ask him out?"

"Oh, right," I scoffed. "I could never do that—call a guy. Could you?"

She hesitated. "No. So much for women's

lib." We both rolled our eyes. Vicky added, "Anyway, Rob's a neat guy. If you like the nerdy type."

I threw the pillow at Vicky, missing her but catching the lavender nail polish full tilt.

"Kaceeeeee!" she screamed, lunging for the airborne bottle and missing it. Instantly, she snatched it up off the floor, but not before a puddle of purple had oozed out all over her brand new white carpet.

I jumped off the bed to clean it up. Vicky held up her hand. "It's okay. I've got it." She wet a cotton ball with polish remover and began to scrub at the purple goo.

"Geez, I'm sorry, Vicky. I'm really sorry."

"It's all right, Kace. I was thinking about moving my desk over here anyway."

Sure, I thought. She'd been begging her mom for years to redecorate her bedroom all in white, although I didn't know another person in the world with a white carpet. I wasn't even sure my bedroom had a floor. I liked to think of it as carpeted in clothes. Anyway, a white carpet didn't seem very practical to me, especially if you had a major klutz for a best friend.

Vicky didn't say it, but I knew she was

upset. We could read each other pretty well after ten years of best friendship.

She must have sensed how awful I felt because she glanced up at me and said, "Kacie, this is not a major catastrophe. Something else is bothering you. What is it?"

I slumped against the bedpost. I wanted to tell her about this morning's little episode in algebra, since it had been preying on my conscience all day. But I didn't want a full-blown lecture on cheating. If Vicky had one fault, it was that she tended to get a little self-righteous at times. You know, holier-than-thou? Besides, it was a one-time thing. My first, and last, offense.

She raised her eyebrows at me.

"It's just been one of those days," I said, shrugging.

Vicky smiled. "Kace, *every* day is one of those days with you." Shaking her head, she added, "I don't know what you'd do without me."

"Die of klutziness, I'm sure," I mumbled.

She pushed up to her feet and tossed the purple cotton balls into the trash. "See?" she said, motioning to the permanently stained spot on the carpet. "It's just like new. Now, do you want me to fix you up for the dance? We could double."

"Oh, right. If one the guys who asked you out ended up with a jerk like me, he'd totally die."

She kicked the bottom of my dangling foot. "Stop putting yourself down. You're more fun than anyone I know. Guys just haven't discovered you yet, that's all. You wait. One day they'll be knocking down your door—"

"Looking for you, no doubt."

Vicky put her hands on her hips. "Kaceeee," she threatened.

Forcing a cheery note to my voice, I said, "So, are you going to show me the dress your mom got you for the dance, or what?"

A smile lit Vicky's face. She bounded like a gazelle to the closet and pulled out a gorgeous, light blue velvet dress. It was trimmed with embroidered lace around the neck and sleeves. *Exactly what a princess would wear*, I thought, watching as she flounced around with the dress in front of the mirror.

"What are you wearing?" she asked.

"One guess," I said, picturing the black

dress I would put on for the bejillionth time. Most of the seams were still intact, plus it gave the illusion I was taller, thinner and my hair was lighter than liverwurst. I figured if I wrapped a scarf around the waist, loaded up on jewelry, wore a paper bag over my head . . . well, it didn't matter to Rob. He never looked at me anyway.

I rose to leave. "I think you should go to the dance with John Masius," I told Vicky. "Dump him after one dance, pick up Phil, and meet Kyle Zimmer in the parking lot afterward. What's the big deal?"

Vicky laughed. "You're hopeless. By the way, I got the bank statement yesterday for our Paris savings account. We made sixty-three cents in interest last month."

"Ooh, double digits," I squealed. "What's our grand total now?"

She sucked in her lips, then exhaled in a laugh. "One hundred twenty-five dollars and eighty-one cents."

"Geez, Vicky. We'll be in our thirties—middle-aged—before we get there."

"We'll get there," she said. "It's our dream, remember?"

Vicky and I had been planning to go to

Paris since fifth grade, when we each got a stuffed French poodle for Christmas. We even took French lessons from a cassette tape. One of the gems I picked up: *"Voulez-vous laver mes chaussettes?"* Translation: "Do you want to wash my socks?" I practiced that for three weeks until Vicky told me what it meant. What can I say? Vicky's always been a little swifter than me.

Vicky waved as I trundled down her front sidewalk and through the chain-link gate. Maybe it was the crisp October air that brought goose bumps to my legs. Or maybe it was my broken sandal strap flapping against my heel. Whatever it was, I shivered and started to zip my jacket. Halfway to my neck the metal clasp broke off in my hand.

Perfect, I thought. *The perfect ending to a zippity doo-dah day.*

Three

I was rummaging through the junk on my locker floor in search of my French text when Skye appeared. "Hi, Kacie," she said. "I have something for you." She handed me a flat box tied with a pink bow.

"What's this?" I asked, my jaw dropping.

"It would be kind of silly to wrap it if I was just going to tell you what was inside," Skye said. "Open it." She smiled coyly.

I removed the ribbon and peeled the tape from the box. Inside, under a mound of pink tissue, lay a beautiful turquoise silk scarf. "Skye," I gasped. "It's . . . fantastic! Why are you giving it to me?"

"You know." She leaned closer. "Because you helped me on the quiz. I got an *A-*, by the way."

"Psychic. Me too."

She cracked up.

Then I said, "You didn't have to get me anything, Skye. Really." The scarf was pretty, though. I thought about how great it would go with my dress for the dance.

Skye lifted the scarf from the box and trailed it around my neck. "I thought you'd like it. It matches your green eyes. Hey, maybe I'll see you at the dance. I'm going with Kyle Zimmer." She wiggled her eyebrows at me.

"Kyle Zimmer? I thought he asked Vicky Anselli."

Skye blinked, then blinked again. "You mean he asked someone else first?"

I cringed, wishing as usual that I had a roll of duct tape to seal my incredibly big mouth. "Maybe I misunderstood," I blundered on. "Maybe it wasn't Kyle *Zimmer*. Maybe it was Kyle . . . Kyle . . ." Ever wonder how a trapped cockroach feels?

Skye forced a knowing smile. "Thanks, Kacie. It doesn't matter. What I really wanted to ask you is, could we study together for the algebra test coming up?

I'm absolutely rotten at math, and you're so good."

Me? Good at math? Good at anything? This was a first—someone asking for *my* help with homework. "Sure, Skye," I said, beaming. "I would be glad to help. When do you want to get together?"

"How about Saturday? I'm free all day."

I wasn't. Vicky and I planned to go shopping. "I can't Saturday. What about Sunday? Like in the afternoon. Unless you have family plans or something."

"Family plans?" Skye gave a short laugh. "No, I don't think I'll have family plans. Any time Sunday is good. We could study at my house. My father will be working, so we'll have the whole place to ourselves."

"That sounds great. How about one o'clock?"

"Super. Here's my address." Skye scrawled it in hot red lipstick on a pale pink sheet of notebook paper and passed it to me. She lived on the outskirts of town, just far enough away to make me not want to walk it unless someone was holding a gun to my head.

"I'll have my mom or dad drive me over," I

said. "Call if things change, like if it turns out that your father doesn't have to work and wants to do something with you." I ripped my own scribbled name from the top of my algebra quiz and added my phone number to the torn sheet.

"Things *won't* change," Skye said. She shoved the scrap of paper with my name and number into her bag. "My father always works on Sundays. Saturdays, Sundays— that's all he ever does—work, work, work . . ." She trailed off, a sad, faraway look in her eyes.

To bring her back I shrugged and said, "Dads are born workaholics. I think it's some kind of mutant gene."

Skye blinked at me once, then burst into laughter. "You're a nut, Kacie," she said, poking my arm. "I have a feeling we're going to be really good friends."

* * * * *

Promptly at seven Friday night, Rob came by my house to get me for the Harvest Dance. I had to admit, he looked hand- some. His dark, curly hair was trimmed over

23

his ears and brushed back in front. Before school started this year, I had talked him into changing his look. He replaced the horn-rimmed nerd specs he usually wore with designer glasses, and he got a better haircut. It helped to set off his deep brown eyes and long, long lashes.

Rob was dressed in a black suit with a turquoise tie, which just happened to match my new scarf perfectly. I was wearing the scarf as a belt. Of course, I had bullied him into buying the tie yesterday after school.

"Hold it." Mom, never one to miss a heartbeat of my growing-up years, grinned and snapped a picture. My baby book was already into volume three and I had barely graduated into my teens. "Perfect," she pronounced. "You two look great."

Dad gave Mom a sappy smile, then turned to us. "Do you two want a ride?" he asked.

"Get real, Dad," I said.

As we trekked off on foot for the three-block walk to Mountain View, Rob said, "You look outstanding, Kacie. I mean it."

Wow. Rob's biggest compliment for anything was to call it "outstanding."

"Thanks, Rob." I smiled up at him. "You look great too."

I'm not sure he heard me. He was staring straight ahead, more distracted than usual. "I'm glad we're going to the dance together," he said. "I wanted to talk to you about something."

It sounded serious. "What?"

Rob cleared his throat. "I . . . I think this is our last date."

What was he saying? Did he have a fatal disease? Was he moving away? Didn't he like my hair?

"I met someone."

Great, I thought. *Just great.*

"Her name is Tanya and she plays the violin. She loves Mozart. You can't imagine what it's like to share my passion."

What did he mean by *that?* I stared at him.

Rob's cheeks blazed. "I mean for Mozart."

"Uh-huh."

"Really, Kacie," Rob said. "She's an outstanding violinist. I met her in the practice room a few weeks ago when we were both working on Jeunehomme, Concerto #9 in E Flat. It was like fate that my piano and her

25

violin joined in a duet." He sighed.

Oh, brother. I glanced sideways at him. He was so lost in another world that when I elbowed him in the ribs, he barely flinched.

"I can't wait for you to meet her, Kacie. You'll really like her. She's just so, so . . ."

"Outstanding?"

"Exactly!" Rob grinned stupidly.

I'd really like her to fiddle around with someone else, I thought. Then I sighed and made myself think the way friends are supposed to think: *Come on, Kacie. You should be happy for him.*

Not entirely without effort, I managed to force a weak smile.

Inside the gym, everyone was paired and rocking to the music that the disc jockey was playing. I spotted Vicky and waved. She had come with John Masius since he had asked her to the dance first. I wondered whether she was thinking about Kyle Zimmer, though. I knew that while Rob and I were dancing, my own thoughts were all over the place. For one thing, I couldn't stop thinking that this might be my last date ever.

During the next slow dance, Rob smiled

at me without really noticing me, and I guessed that his mind must be on Tanya. I suddenly realized he had given up a romantic evening with her for a crummy friendship date with me. I dragged him over to the punch bowl. "Rob, you didn't have to bring me to the dance, you know. You could have asked Tanya."

He shifted uncomfortably. "I wanted to bring you. I owe a lot to you, Kacie— probably my whole social existence."

That was true. When Rob moved to Lafayette three years earlier, he had a hard time adjusting. Everyone assumed he was a major nerd since he'd transferred from a private academy in the East. Plus, he *looked* like a nerd. It didn't help that whenever he spoke to people he used hundred-syllable words. I concluded that because he was a musical genius, his parents had severely sheltered him. So I took him under my wing, got him to update his look, and taught him about geeks, punks, stoners and all. Generally, I showed him how to survive in public school. In the process we became really close friends.

I sipped cloudy red punch from a paper

cup and looked up at Rob. He was staring down at me. With a gulp he said, "I wanted to break this to you gently, about Tanya. It won't affect our friendship."

Oh, sure, I thought.

"But it's time I spread my wings a little," Rob continued. "You know, moved to a higher plane?"

"So you could drop a bomb on me?"

He made a face. "You know what I mean."

I shrugged.

"Come on, Kace. You know how I feel about you." He took my hand.

"Then dump Tanya."

He dropped my hand like a live grenade. "That's like asking me to give up Mozart!"

"Horrors!" I clenched my throat. The shock on his face made me burst into laughter. "I'm only kidding, Rob. I think it's great." I punched his arm. "Thanks for bringing me tonight. You're a good friend. And I'm glad about Tanya. I am. Really. I mean it."

Who was I trying to convince here?

*   *   *   *   *

The next morning I got up early to meet Vicky. I mean, nine o'clock on a Saturday is serious. Our plan was to spend the entire day shopping at the Boulder Mall, using what was left of our summer babysitting money. We always babysat together, not only to keep each other company, but as a way to make sure neither of us strangled the really obnoxious kids.

I always looked forward to our shopping sprees, especially when we had finally set aside enough money to actually buy something valuable, like a new pair of jeans. Plus, I couldn't wait to hear if she had enjoyed herself at the dance with John.

When I arrived at her house, Vicky was just coming out the front door. "What timing," I said. "If we hurry we can catch the next bus."

"Kacie!" she gasped. "Oh, no."

"Oh, no? What? Did I spill something on this top too?" I checked my shirt for grape stains.

She swallowed hard. "I'm sorry. I forgot to tell you, I have a special cheerleading practice today. It's for the state competition, you know? I forgot all about shopping."

29

Thanks a lot, Vicky, I thought to myself. *We've only been planning this for a month.* "When does practice end?" I asked, trying not to show how annoyed I was. "Maybe we could meet later."

Vicky shook her head. "I signed up to cheer at the junior varsity football game afterward. I'm sorry." She smiled apologetically. "Look, why don't we go next Saturday? Shop till we drop?"

"Okay," I said, shrugging so it wouldn't look like it mattered. "Call me tonight? I really want to hear about the dance. We didn't get to talk even once last night. Did you have fun?"

She nodded. "I really did. John isn't Kyle Zimmer, but he's nice, and he *did* invite me first. I tried to snag you a couple of times at the refreshment table, but you and Rob were into some heavy discussion."

"Yeah, and wait till you hear—"

"I'm late, Kace. Gotta run. Sorry." Then, as an afterthought, Vicky asked, "Did you have a good time?"

"Yeah, but—"

"Terrific." Vicky started to sprint toward school.

"Call me later," I yelled after her.

She waved over her shoulder. "I will. I promise."

I stayed by the phone all evening. She never called.

Four

I knew Vicky would be at church Sunday morning, so I didn't even try to call her. At quarter to one I phoned, but there was no answer. By then I had to leave for Skye's or I would be really late.

Dad drove me across town to Skye's house. Actually, it was more like an estate, at least compared to our puny pre-fab. A six-foot-high stone wall bordered the grounds. I rechecked the lipstick address Skye had given me. The brass numerals on the ornamental iron gate matched perfectly.

Dad whistled. "Upscaling, are we?"

I widened my eyes in awed response while he drove through the gate and followed a circular drive. At the end of the drive, enormous carved doors burst apart and Skye appeared in the doorway. She ran down the steps to greet us.

"Wow, Kacie. Your dad's really handsome," she whispered, loud enough for him to hear.

Dad looked kind of embarrassed, so I said, "Yeah, he gets his looks from me," and he cracked up.

After a quick kiss on the cheek, Dad reminded me that he'd be back around five. I watched him rumble off in our old station wagon, drive around the cul-de-sac, through the gate and out of view.

Skye grabbed my arm and pulled me into the house. "I'm so glad you're here," she said.

All I could do was gape. "Your house is . . . is . . ." What was bigger than awesome and outrageous?

"It's okay," Skye said. "I liked the house I grew up in better. This one is so, I don't know, sterile."

Yeah, it looked squeaky clean to me. Skye's dad probably had an army of maids in the servants' quarters. "You didn't tell me you were rich," I said.

Skye laughed. "We're not rich. My dad is a congressman. You know how much *they* make." She tossed her hair breezily over her shoulder as she bounded away across the marble floor.

No, I didn't know how much they made, but it was obviously a whole lot more than Dad, who was a tax accountant. I tagged behind Skye, scanning the vaulted ceilings and shimmering skylights. "Do you have brothers and sisters?" I asked.

"Nope," Skye said over her shoulder. "There's just me and Daddy. Most of the time it's just me. Except today, it's me and you." Her eyes lit up. "Come on, let's have lunch." Skye tugged at my arm and led me down a seemingly endless hallway to the kitchen.

So what if I'd already eaten? Skye pulled out two gigantic, already-assembled submarine sandwiches.

"The only good thing about living here," she said as she nuked the sandwiches in the microwave, "is that there's a stable next door where I can go and ride whenever I want. In fact, I had a riding lesson scheduled this afternoon, but I canceled it since you were coming."

"Geez, Skye. You didn't have to do that." I couldn't believe she had actually changed her plans for me—unlike a certain best friend of mine who shall remain nameless.

Climbing onto a stool at the breakfast counter, I said, "I didn't see you at the Harvest Dance Friday night. I saw Kyle a couple of times, but you weren't with him."

Skye bit into her sandwich. "I decided not to go at the last minute," she said, her words muffled. Then she took a swig from a soda can. "Kyle Zimmer's not that big of a deal."

"You've got to be kidding!" I said. "He's the hottest—" The eye bullets she shot at me said to drop that subject out of state. I chomped into my sandwich.

Skye chattered on about school and teachers—you know, surface stuff—while we finished our sandwiches and drinks. Then she pulled out all the ingredients to make brownies. Hey, there's always room for brownies, and Skye didn't exactly have to twist my arm for help. But later, when I was finally pulling the tray out of the oven, I heard muted chimes from a grandfather clock somewhere off in another section of the house. "Skye," I said, "maybe we should start studying now. It's already three o'clock."

Skye gasped. "Three o'clock? I haven't even shown you my music collection."

We carried a plate of brownies up the stairs to Skye's room at the end of the hall. Her bedroom was the size of our entire family room, I swear. She had a bed with a canopy, an enormous walk-in closet, and enough sound equipment to stage a concert.

Her tape collection was awesome. She had all the classics: Ixtapa, Thrush, and Jean Pool, plus a lot of my favorites, including Tiara, the Technotics, Ariki Rin, and XLR8. She asked me to pick, so I shoved the newest release from the Technotics into her player.

Geez, it was loud. There must have been hidden speakers in the walls. Skye suddenly grabbed my wrist and we danced and giggled for about an hour, until I remembered why I was there.

"Skye, are we ever going to study?" I asked.

She sprawled across the bed. "I don't

feel like it, do you?"

I laughed. That was a dumb question. I inserted the next tape as Skye bounded to her feet and raced downstairs for some more drinks.

While a blast of chords from XLR8 electrified the air, I looked around Skye's room. You could tell a lot about people by studying their stuff. First off, Skye's room was a total disaster area. It was nice to know someone else appreciated the beauty of chaos. Her closet was jam-packed with clothes and shoes and accessories.

There was a gorgeous, pastel portrait of Skye on the wall. It showed off her brilliant blue eyes and amber hair—nothing like the blurry photo blow-up of me on our living room wall.

Skye's dresser was stacked with makeup and hair products. Jewelry was tossed helter-skelter, just the way I liked mine sorted. On her bureau lay a pile of money, and it wasn't pocket change. I counted thirty dollars, and that was just the top layer. Next to the money was a picture in a silver frame. When I picked it up to examine it more closely, a hand reached around to yank it away.

"What were you doing with that?" Skye demanded sharply.

"Geez, you scared me." I felt my heart do a little gallop. "I was just looking at it. Sorry. Who is it, anyway?"

Skye took a deep breath. "My mother."

"Really?" I peered over the top of the frame to get a closer look. "She's beautiful," I said. "You know, you look a lot like her."

"She *was* beautiful," said Skye. She locked her eyes on me. "She's dead now."

I caught my breath. "Oh, Skye. I'm sorry. How did she—"

"Car accident. Her car spun out of control on the ice and hit a tree. She died instantly."

How horrible! And how awful to have to tell people who couldn't learn to keep their big mouths shut. "It must be really hard on your father," I said.

"I wouldn't know. We don't discuss it. All I know is—" Skye inhaled a shaky breath "— I really miss her."

"Oh, Skye. I'm sorry." I touched her shoulder gently.

She shook her head. *"I'm* sorry, Kacie. I

didn't mean to snap at you. It just hurts to think about her." A second later Skye tossed the picture into a drawer and slammed it shut. "Let's change the subject, okay? Do you like Marina and the Mix?"

"Uh, sure."

"Good, I'll add it to the stack." Suddenly, Skye thrust a bunch of tapes into my hands. "Here. These are for you."

"What? No, I can't!" I realized that Skye had been setting aside all the tapes I had picked out during the afternoon. Now she was giving them to me. I tried to give them back, but she wouldn't let me.

"I want you to have them," Skye said firmly. "Look, I have enough to listen to for the rest of my life." She waved a hand toward her collection. "And if I miss one of these, I'll just come and listen to it at your house. You're the nicest person I've met since I moved here."

I felt my face heat up.

"Please take them, Kacie. You'll hurt my feelings if you don't."

Wow. I felt uncomfortable about this. Weird, even. But I had never hurt anyone's feelings on purpose. And I guessed it was okay to accept presents from Skye for no reason. It's not like I had done anything wrong this time. Actually, maybe this was sort of like charity. I could live with that. I mean, I hadn't begged for the tapes. Still, it didn't feel right and finally I said, "I can't take all of these, Skye. It's too many."

"Then choose one. Pick out your favorite."

"Well . . . I do like Tiara."

"It's yours." Skye dropped the tape into my book bag, along with four or five others, but who was counting?

A little while later Dad arrived to pick me up. I waved goodbye to Skye and climbed into the car beside him.

"So, did you get a lot of studying done?" he asked while slowing the car at the gate.

"There wasn't much time after lunch. And brownies. And dancing."

Dad chuckled, but it sounded kind of forced. Then he said, "You know, Kacie, I've never interfered with your choice of friends before, but I have to say there's something about this girl I don't like. I don't know . . . she just seems phony."

"Dad, you don't even know her!"

He took a minute to answer. "I guess I've just learned to trust my instincts about people. Maybe being an accountant gives me more exposure to the deceitful side of people. I don't know. Just be careful. Okay, honey? Don't let her buy your friendship."

"Dad, what an awful thing to say," I complained, avoiding his laserlike gaze. "Just because she has a little bit of money." While I tightened the grip on my book bag, I thought, *what could a couple of old cassette tapes be worth, anyway?*

Five

ROB called to ask if I would meet him at the Dairy Kreme after school the next day. The DK was the middle school hangout, and even on a Monday, by the time I arrived it was already packed. I spotted Rob's hair above a booth and weaved my way through the crowd. It wasn't until I reached the table that I noticed he wasn't alone.

"Kacie, meet Tanya Muniz. Tanya, Kacie Shannon."

"Hi," I said. Tanya pushed wire-rimmed glasses up her nose and smiled through thin lips.

Rob scooted to the other side of the circular booth so I could sit next to Tanya. *Thanks a lot, Rob,* I thought. "Rob tells me you play the fiddle," I said to Tanya.

Tanya choked on her shake. Rob glared at me. "I mean the violin," I said. "He says you're really good. Have you been playing a long time?"

She nodded. "Since I was three."

"Years old? Geez. Were you even potty trained?"

Rob kicked me under the table. I added quickly, "You must be good by now."

"She's outstanding," Rob said as he dug into his hot fudge sundae. He glanced up at me. "Do you want something to eat, Kace?"

"Sure, just the usual—you know." My usual was a Butterfinger Blitz. I didn't really want one, so I must have said that just to irk Tanya. I can be so mean sometimes. Rob slid around the booth and out the other side.

Tanya slurped on her shake. Besides her interest in music, I wondered what the attraction was for Rob. She seemed so—I don't know—boring, with her short straight hair and glasses. She even wore a black skirt and white blouse, buttoned clear up to the neck.

Suddenly I felt self-conscious in my

glittery hooped earrings, silver jangle belt, and fire engine-red sweater. I pushed the frizzed-out pony tail over my ear a little closer to my head.

Tanya cleared her throat. "How long have you known Rob?" she asked.

I shrugged. "About three years. We pretty much shared puberty." Tanya coughed and I slapped her on the back.

Rob set the Blitz down in front of me. "You owe me," he said, slipping back into place.

"Put it on my tab." I downed a spoonful of the thick, orange-brown glop.

"Do you play an instrument?" Tanya asked, dabbing what little there was of her lips with a napkin.

"Yeah."

Rob's eyes widened.

I widened mine back at him. "I sing."

Rob smirked. He and I shared a grin. Tanya noticed.

"Actually," I said, "I had a Mickey Mouse guitar when I was five. Mom and Dad thought I had real potential."

She asked seriously, "You didn't keep it up?"

"No. Most of the strings broke when I left it outside all winter. And it had this kind of gritty sound after the dog buried it in the backyard."

Rob laughed. Tanya frowned. I sucked up another spoonful of the Blitz.

"Hi, you guys." Vicky burst through the crowd. She was wearing her cheerleader uniform and licking a two-scoop ice cream cone. "Slide over," she said, rustling her pom-pom at me.

As she pushed in beside me, Rob said, "Vicky, this is Tanya Muniz. Tanya, Vicky Anselli."

"Hi," Vicky said. "Are you new here?"

Tanya nodded. "I transferred from Broomfield. The music program is better at Mountain View. Not to mention," she added, batting her eyes at Rob, "the musicians."

I choked. Rob's cheeks reddened. He smiled and wrapped his arm around Tanya's shoulders. Vomitose.

"Rob's girlfriend," I whispered to Vicky.

"You didn't tell me," she whispered back. Before I could respond, she said, "Hey, did you guys hear someone broke into the copy room at school, and like, totally trashed the place?"

Rob, Tanya, and I all gaped at her. "You're kidding," I said. "What for?"

Vicky said, "I don't know exactly, but someone told me that teachers sometimes keep their test answers in a filing cabinet in there. Maybe some slimeball was trying to cheat." She shook her head. "There's nothing worse than cheating. Except maybe lying about it."

Why was she looking at me?

"Hi, Vicky. Can I sit down?" Kyle Zimmer appeared through a gap in the crowd.

"Sure." Vicky pinched me hard on the leg.

"I've been meaning to call you," he said. "Sorry about asking you to the dance so late. I should have figured you'd have a waiting line."

Vicky pinched me again. If she didn't quit it she was going to experience a Butterfinger Blitz on the head.

"Are you busy Friday night?" he asked her. "There's a bunch of us going to the Razz—you know, that new under-sixteen dance club?" He flashed a brilliant smile at her.

If her cone wasn't melting, my

Blitz definitely was.

"Sounds like fun," she said casually.

I would have been out of there, dressed and waiting by the door.

"Great," said Kyle. "I'll pick you up at seven. No, make that six. We can stop for Italian." He smiled again, then inched a little closer to Vicky. "I hear you're trying out for Guinevere in the school play," he said. "I can't believe we're actually doing *Camelot* this year, can you? I'm going to try out for King Arthur."

"You are?" Vicky's eyes lit up as she daintily licked her cone. I swear that ice cream would have been dripping down my wrists by then.

"I hope you get the part," she said. "I haven't really decided if I want to try out. I'm kind of scared." She turned her shoulders toward him, and her back to me.

"Don't be scared. I'll coach you," he said.

I shifted, elbowing her in the side accidentally on purpose. Then I tuned back in to Rob's conversation with Tanya. They were still talking music, of course, totally oblivious to everyone else. "Do you think I should play that glissando in the Hungarian

47

Rhapsody more dolce or forte?" he asked her.

Oh, brother. I rolled my eyes as I spooned in another glob of Blitz. Vicky rose to leave with Kyle. I caught her arm.

"Hey, Vicky. Will you help me with my algebra test?"

"Sure," she said. "When is it?"

"Tomorrow."

She frowned. "Tonight I'm cheering at a football game and then I have a paper to write for my English class. Tomorrow there's an early morning meeting for the new Fun Committee—you know, that club I was telling you about for organizing all the socials? Do you want to join with me?"

"What time's the meeting?"

"Seven."

"A.M.?" I shook my head. "No, thanks. I'll probably be studying." Actually, I would probably be sleeping.

"Well, sorry, Kace," said Vicky. "You should have called me yesterday. I was free all afternoon." Kyle grabbed her hand and pulled her into the crowd. "Call me later," she yelled over her shoulder.

Rob and Tanya slid out of the booth.

"Nice to meet you, Tracey." Tanya pushed her glasses up her nose.

"Kacie." I forced a grin. Rob smiled at her with adoring eyes. Before they disappeared into the mob, he hollered over his shoulder, "I'll call you later . . . Tracey."

A blob of Blitz ran down my chin. "I'll get you for that, Rob! I swear I'll get you."

Six

MY alarm blared. With a major groan, I flung the nearest object at it—my algebra book. I had stayed up past midnight factoring equations and I felt run down, like an electronic game with worn-out batteries. With a half-open eye I peered across the room at the numbers glowing on my digital clock: eight . . . zero . . . zero.

Mom pounded on the door. "Hurry up, Kacie. You're going to be late."

Grumbling, I rolled out of bed and quickly showered and dressed. On the way to school I scarfed down a peanut butter granola bar. Still half-asleep and mumbling, "6Y minus 8Z pluhzzzzzzzz," I slid into my desk at the back of the room.

Oh Tannenbaum rattled off the directions while she passed out the tests. Skye smiled at me as she cleared her desk. "Good luck," she whispered.

I felt my whole body tighten. Some people have test anxiety. I have test-o-phobia. I know because I have all the symptoms—nausea, dizziness, and an uncontrollable urge to chew erasers. I inhaled deeply and began the test.

A few minutes later, Skye's pencil clattered to the floor. Out of the corner of my eye I saw her lean over and pull something from her purse. My mind was on Problem Three, and I didn't think anything of it. Then, just as I began to work on the second page, I felt a tap on my shoulder.

I looked up to see Skye's eyes focused not on me, but on Oh Tannenbaum, who was pacing at the front of the room. When our algebra teacher ambled down the far aisle to answer a question, Skye sneaked a folded sheet of paper onto my desk. Oh Tannenbaum had her back to us, so I unfolded the sheet.

My mouth dropped to the floor. For a few seconds I just sat there, staring. When I glanced over at Skye, she winked.

The paper held all the answers to the problems. The copy was poor, but it was unmistakably Oh Tannenbaum's handwriting. My heart did a major drum roll. All I had to do was copy the rest of the problems, make sure the ones I had already completed were correct and—no! I wasn't a cheater. Quickly, I refolded the paper and thrust it back at Skye.

"Kacie? What is that?" Oh Tannenbaum's massive body loomed over me. "May I have it, please?" She held out a thick hand.

I squeezed my eyes shut and handed the paper over.

You've never seen such a major fit. Oh Tannenbaum paraded me to the door in front of everyone. From behind, I heard the whole class jeering, "Ooh, Kacie. Busted." I could have died.

After a long march down a long hall to the principal's office, Oh Tannenbaum slammed the confiscated answer sheet on Dr. Sandoval's desk. While our principal studied it, Oh Tannenbaum just stood there, arms folded, foot tapping.

Dr. Sandoval lowered her glasses. "Kacie,

where did you get this?" she asked.

"I, uh . . . I found it." Well, that wasn't exactly a lie. I found it on my desk. "But I didn't use it," I said. "Honest."

Oh Tannenbaum snorted.

In desperation I added, "Just look at my test. You can see I didn't copy the answers."

"Is that true?" Dr. Sandoval glanced up at my algebra teacher. Oh Tannenbaum huffed, then grudgingly looked over my test.

"Well, yes. I guess it is. I didn't notice it before. I just assumed—"

"Thank you, Mrs. Tannenbaum," said Dr. Sandoval. "I'd like to talk to Kacie alone for a few minutes."

Oh Tannenbaum scowled at me, then lumbered off.

Dr. Sandoval furrowed her brow. Her gray eyes were fixed on my face. "Kacie, tell me," she began, "how did this get into your possession?"

"I . . . I told you. I found it." I dropped my eyes to my lap and began to fidget with a thumbnail.

She settled back in her chair. "I assume you heard about the copy room break-in. We weren't exactly sure

53

what was taken until now."

"I didn't do it!" My head whipped up.

"I'm not accusing you. I know you, Kacie. And I don't believe for a second that you did it. But I'd like to know who you're protecting. And why. Do you think it's right for someone to steal test answers and cheat on exams?"

I met her gaze. "Of course not."

"Then why is it worth protecting the guilty party?"

Sometimes there's just no answer for things. I honestly couldn't explain why I was covering up for Skye. I only knew I had to.

Dr. Sandoval sighed. "All right, Kacie. I'm going to forget it this time. But please tell your so-called friend that he or she almost put *you* on suspension."

The principal rose to her feet and brushed past me to open the door. My knees buckled under her disapproving eyes as I slinked out around her.

Back at my locker Skye was pacing nervously. When she spotted me she rushed up and grabbed my arm. "What happened?"

"Oh, I almost got suspended, that's all."

She looked horrified. "I'm so sorry,

Kacie. It's all my fault."

"Skye, did you steal those test answers from the copy room?" I asked her point-blank.

She blinked at me. "No. But the guy who did was selling the answers, so I bought them. I had to."

I shook my head. This was unbelievable. "Why?" I asked. "Why did you 'have' to?"

"For you," she answered.

"Me?"

"I didn't want to be responsible for you failing the test. I mean, I forced you to make brownies and listen to tapes instead of studying." Skye's eyes filled with tears. "I was only trying to help."

Forced me to make brownies and listen to tapes. Right. I took a deep breath. "I'm sorry, Skye. I know you were trying to help, but geez."

She lifted her head and looked at me. "I only thought since you cheated on the last one . . ."

I flinched. I had almost forgotten about the quiz. I guess I had convinced myself that giving someone else the answers wasn't cheating, but of course it was. I didn't want

Skye to get the wrong idea about me, though. "Look Skye, I don't know why I gave you my quiz to copy. I've never done that before. Not for anyone. I guess I just felt like you needed help. But it was a one-time thing, okay?"

Skye slumped back against the lockers. "Great," she mumbled. "I guess that means you told Dr. Sandoval the truth. My dad's going to kill me when he finds out."

"He won't," I said. "I didn't tell Dr. Sandoval anything."

"You didn't?" Skye's eyes grew wide. "Why not?"

"Because . . . because you don't rat on your friends, okay? It's just one of those unwritten laws."

"Oh, Kacie!" Skye pushed off from the lockers. "No one has ever done anything like this for me before. I mean, taken the blame. That's serious. You don't know how much I appreciate it." Without warning, she threw her arms around me in a bone-crunching hug.

"Can we just forget it?" I said, loosening her grip. I wasn't exactly feeling noble.

"Well, I'm not going to forget it," Skye

replied. "You're a fantastic friend." I heard her say to herself, "This calls for something really special." Then, with a winning smile, she added, "I'll catch you later." She waved lightly and bounded off down the hall.

"Skye, please! No gifts!" I called after her, but my plea was lost in the crush of kids charging down the hall between classes.

Vicky rounded the corner beside Kyle. "Hi, Kace." She stopped at my locker. "How was your algebra test?" Kyle whispered something in her ear and she giggled, punching him in the ribs.

"Oh," I said, "it was easy, like I had all the answers right at my fingertips. Listen, Vicky. Can I talk to you for a minute?" I needed to confide in her about this. I needed her to help me sort out my feelings.

Vicky glanced at her watch. "I'll be late for English. Can we catch up to each other later, Kace? Maybe after school. Oh, wait. I have cheerleading practice tonight." Kyle pulled her back into the crowd. "I'll call you when I get home." Vicky smiled over her shoulder and waved. "I promise."

*　*　*　*　*

Right after dinner I gave her a call. I wasn't going to wait for her to break another promise. "Vicky, you wouldn't believe what happened to me today—"

"Kacie, I'm dead," she said, cutting me off. "I've had the worst headache all afternoon. Can this wait until tomorrow? I really need to go to bed for, like, *forever.*"

I felt my whole body sag. "Sure, Vicky," I said softly. "It can wait. It's not important. I hope you feel better."

"Thanks. Good night."

The dial tone broke the connection between us.

Seven

OUR algebra tests were returned the next day. Adorning the top of my paper was a big fat *D*. Most of the problems I had completed before my capture were correct, but I hadn't finished even a third of the exam. Skye gave me a weak smile as she jammed her paper into her bag. I glimpsed her grade, though: *B+*. Where was the justice?

I was so upset I tried to sneak out after class. But Skye caught up with me in the hall and stayed right on my heels. "Algebra is such a waste," she complained.

"I don't understand why you didn't get an *A*," I snapped, rounding a corner at high speed.

"Oh, Kacie," she said, "it would be too obvious if I answered every question right. I always make sure to miss a few."

I skidded to a halt and looked at Skye point-blank. "You mean you've cheated before?"

She gulped. "Well, uh . . . I don't want to lie to you. I have. But it was a long time ago, last year. After my mother . . ." She lowered her eyes. "I couldn't concentrate on anything after the accident. I was so desperate, I knew if I didn't cheat, I'd flunk math. It's my worst subject. Daddy would have been furious." She swallowed hard. "You don't know him, Kacie. He would ground me for months if I came home with an *F*."

"I'm sorry, Skye." I shook my head. "I know it must have been awful for you, but cheating still isn't right. If you need help in school, why don't you go to the tutoring center? Or find someone to study with?"

"You're right," said Skye. "That's what I need to do. I know I can't handle it by myself. Can you come over on Saturday? You can be my tutor. We have all those chapters to do before the midterm."

"I'm sorry," I said, "but I can't. Vicky and

I are going shopping." *If I rate over cheer-leading practice this time,* I added to myself.

"Vicky Anselli? The pom-pom girl? You mean she's a friend of yours?" Skye's face lost all expression.

"She's been my best friend since just about forever."

"Oh." In a flat voice Skye said, "Well, okay then. Forget it. I guess if you can't come, I'll study by myself. But I know I can't do it. I'll just get an *F*." She took a deep breath and looked away. "My dad's going to ground me for life. But so what?"

So what? I didn't want that.

I understood about not being able to do it. The only reason my grades were even halfway decent was because of Vicky's help. I sighed. "Okay, I'll come, Skye," I said. "Just let me work it out with Vicky. Hey, maybe after we're done shopping in the morning, she could come, too. She's a total brain. She always helps me with my homework —"

"No way," she said, cutting me off. "Just you, Kacie."

"What do you have against Vicky?" I asked, frowning.

"Nothing. It's just that, well, two's company, three's a crowd. Isn't that some kind of unwritten law?" Skye flashed a sudden smile. "Oh, I almost forgot. I have something for you." She reached into her bag and pulled out a small box.

I held up my hand. "Not another present, Skye. I can't accept it."

"Come on, Kacie. I need to make up for yesterday. I feel so guilty about getting you into trouble. Please? It's no big deal."

My ability to say no was weaker than overcooked spaghetti. The box was gray velveteen and small. When I popped it open, I gasped. Inside was a delicate gold chain, all wound up. As I uncoiled it, a tiny gold heart swung free from the middle.

"Skye, it's beautiful!" I said.

"Here, put it on." Skye helped me remove my blue plastic beads, the ones I had splurged a nickel on at a garage sale.

"Gorgeous!" she exclaimed. She whipped a compact out of her purse and held up its mirror for me to confirm.

The gold shimmered under the fluorescent hall light. "It's beautiful, Skye. But I just can't accept—"

Skye snapped her compact closed and dropped it in her bag. Then she disappeared down the hall before I could even think about giving the necklace back.

*   *   *   *   *

There was a virus of some sort going around and Vicky caught it. She was out of school all day Thursday. I stopped by her house after school, but she was asleep. It seemed weird, not even talking on the phone to her. I was reminded of the time we had been separated for an entire week. It was the Christmas vacation she spent with her grandparents in Chicago. I thought I would die of boredom before she finally got back.

Fortunately, Vicky came back to life on Friday. After school she showed up on my doorstep, out of breath and hysterical. "Help!" she cried. "Kyle's taking me dancing at the Razz in three hours and I don't have a thing to wear."

I was so glad to see her functioning that I practically knocked her down pulling her into the house. "You can wear anything that doesn't look better on you than it does on me," I said. "Kind of limits it, huh? Anyway, I'm sure I have just gobs of outfits for a dance club date with the second hottest guy in school."

She raised her eyebrows. "Second?"

"Daniel Oakes."

"Oh, right. I forgot." She laughed. We went to my room and Vicky surveyed my closet, along with the larger land mass of clothes on my floor. She held up wrinkled skirts, stretch pants, jeans, sweaters, and dresses. We decided my most appealing outfit was a pair of faded jeans shorts with a polka dot halter top. Perfect for October in Colorado.

"Maybe I'll just borrow some jewelry," Vicky said. When she opened my jewelry box, the gold heart necklace sparkled under the light. Vicky gasped. "Where did you get this?"

"Uh, from a friend," I stammered. Before I could shovel my cheap stuff over the top of it, Vicky had picked it up.

"It looks expensive, Kacie. What kind of friend? Like a boyfriend?"

"Get real. I just did someone a favor and she gave me a present."

"Must have been some favor. Mind if I

wear it?" She pressed the necklace against her neck in front of the mirror.

"Well, actually, I do," I said, pulling it away from her. I tossed it back into the jewelry box and slammed the lid. The hurt on Vicky's face hurt me, and I had to turn away.

I don't know why I didn't want her to wear the necklace. Okay, maybe I did. It wasn't exactly a gift I was proud of receiving. *And* I was afraid of what Vicky might say about my new friendship with Skye, especially if it got out that she had bought those test answers. Vicky and I had never kept secrets from each other before. But I think that in the back of my mind I was a little ticked off at her for being so out of touch lately, and maybe this was my way of getting back. Real nice, huh?

While I was still sorting out my feelings I heard her say, "You got the new Tiara tape! You never told me, you rat. When did you buy it?" She inserted the tape into my player, then faced me, waiting for an answer.

I forced a half-smile, and cranked the volume up real loud so that we couldn't talk. So that I wouldn't have to tell her the truth.

Eight

I called Vicky first thing Saturday morning to pin down our shopping plans. I also wanted to find out about her date with Kyle. Mostly, I just wanted to talk. I felt increasingly guilty about the necklace, and keeping secrets, and for more or less blaming her for being popular and perfect. I had called Skye earlier to arrange our study session for two o'clock. That way I'd have all morning to spend with Vicky. I planned to tell her everything while we were shopping. I wanted to totally clear the air.

Mrs. Anselli answered the phone. "Oh, hi, Kacie. Vicky's still in bed," she said. "She got in pretty late last night. As soon as she gets up, I'll tell her you called."

Half an hour later, I couldn't stand it any more. I called again. Vicky wasn't there. She had taken off for pom-pom practice. She never even returned my call! Once again, our shopping plans were blown out of the water. I couldn't believe she had just forgotten.

Since I didn't have anything else to do now—like confide my deepest feelings to my best friend—I moped around all morning, forced to either clean my room or do homework. I cleaned my room. At noon Dad said he was driving over to the hardware store, so I asked him to drop me off at Skye's. Okay, I was a little early—only about two hours.

When we arrived I spotted a silver Mercedes in the driveway. A man in a pin-striped suit was just walking toward it as Dad and I pulled up. When he saw our car, he turned and headed toward us. He looked puzzled.

"Can I help you with something?" he asked, peering into Dad's window.

"I was just dropping my daughter off and—" Suddenly, Dad inclined his head. "Charles?" he asked, surprise in his voice.

He yanked up the emergency brake and we both stepped out of the car. "Well, I'll be darned. This is like seeing a ghost from my past."

A second later the man said, "Steve?" A smile of recognition crossed his face. He and Dad shook hands. "It's been years! In fact, I don't think I've seen you since college. Unbelievable!"

Dad laughed and said, "Charles 'Chug-A-Lug' Collinsworth. I didn't make the connection when Kacie mentioned your daughter's name."

Mr. Collinsworth laughed too. "I'd forgotten about my disreputable reputation. I wish you would too." They both laughed. "So this is your daughter?"

"Kacie." Dad beamed at me.

"Hello, Kacie." Mr. Collinsworth held out his hand.

"Hi," I mumbled. My hand disappeared into his. Just then Skye materialized at the front door of the house. As politely as I could, I excused myself and bounded up the steps.

"Hi, Skye. Looks like your dad and mine are old pals."

"Really? Too bad they didn't stay in

touch. We could have been friends a long time ago."

We both looked at our dads. They were chuckling and telling old stories. Then they shook hands again. Dad waved to me as he started toward the car. "I'll be back at five to pick you up, honey."

"Nonsense," Mr. Collinsworth said. "We'll bring Kacie home on our way to dinner." He addressed his daughter. "I'll be back in a few hours, Skye. Please stay home. The Baxters have invited us to an early dinner, so you'll need to be ready by four-thirty. Wear something nice. It's important that we make a good impression tonight. Jonathan Baxter is very influential in the district."

He said to Dad, "I'll sure be glad when this election is over, win or lose. If I have to raise one more dollar by eating stuffed croquettes with stuffed shirts . . ." He sighed.

Dad said, "You could always come over to my place and stuff yourself with meatloaf."

Mr. Collinsworth laughed. "I told you lawyers made more than bean counters, but you wouldn't listen."

"Must have been the beans in my ears." Dad shrugged. "Anyway, from my vantage point, success is measured in a lot of different ways." He looked at me and winked.

I groaned to myself.

Mr. Collinsworth glanced at his watch. "Good to see you, Steve. I'm sorry I've got to run. Maybe we can meet for lunch when my schedule settles down a bit."

Mr. Collinsworth slid in behind the wheel of his car and revved up the motor. Dad did the same, but puffs of black smoke spewed from his exhaust pipe. I could have died. The sleek silver Mercedes hummed down the driveway with Dad sputtering behind in the crusty old station wagon.

All right, this was too weird. Skye's father wasn't at all the creep I'd imagined him to be. He was a little stiff, true, and he seemed kind of tense. But he was nice enough.

Before I could utter a word, Skye grabbed my arm and pulled me inside. "He sure lays it on thick, doesn't he?" she said.

"What do you mean?"

"Daddy's a politician, remember? He's always got to bring up what he does. Sometimes I wish he'd just lose the election. Then maybe we could be a family again."

"Skye! You don't mean that."

"Don't I?" She hesitated, like maybe she really did. Then she sighed and shook her head. "Men."

"Really." I rolled my eyes sympathetically.

Skye smiled. "I'm glad you came early, Kacie. I've been going stir-crazy all morning. I even went to the library just to get out of here for a while. Can you believe it? The *library?* What happened, anyway? I thought you were going shopping with Vicky."

"Change of plans," I muttered.

She looked at me. Then she gave me an understanding squeeze on the shoulder.

We climbed the long staircase to her room and she told me to pick out a tape while she changed clothes. I didn't know why she was changing. I mean, we were only going to study. As I inserted the tape and adjusted the volume on her stereo, she flung her cashmere sweater across the room and pulled on a different one. Next, she flopped onto her vanity seat, opened a tube of lipstick and spread royal red all over her lips. She examined her image in the mirror, pouted, blotted her lips with a Kleenex, and tossed the tube over her shoulder. It cracked me up, and we both started to giggle.

While she was rummaging around for more lipstick, I was thinking that her room looked like a tornado had just blown through. I noticed the picture of her mother was back on the dresser.

Suddenly, Skye bolted from her seat. She flicked off the stereo and tugged at my hand. "Come on. Let's go."

"Go where?" I asked.

"Shopping, of course. I thought you wanted to go shopping."

"I did, but . . . I thought we were here to study."

"Study? On a Saturday? Are you a Eugene?"

I'd never been called a Eugene, didn't exactly know what it meant, but it sounded plenty disgusting. Skye coaxed me toward the door. Truth is, it didn't take much coaxing. "What about what your father said?" I asked.

"The bus to Boulder stops right outside the gate," she replied. "We can go and be back in plenty of time. He won't even know we left. Ready?"

"I, uh, didn't bring any money."

"Don't worry," said Skye. She hoisted an

oversized purse onto her shoulder. "I have some. And Daddy owes me my allowance for this week."

She took my arm and ushered me down the stairs. Maybe I should have resisted, but I didn't. And I don't think I could have talked her out of going, anyway. When Skye made up her mind, it was, like, already history.

She opened the double doors to her father's study and marched in. It was a fantastic room, with some kind of expensive-looking wood paneling and massive furniture to match. Oriental carpeting gave it a majorly rich feeling. One entire wall was lined with books, and there was even a high-tech copy machine in the corner. It reminded me of all those rooms you see on TV murder mysteries.

My sneakers sank into the carpet as I followed Skye. She crossed the room and pushed a secret button on the side of a huge bookcase. Silently, one floor-to-wall section of the bookcase opened. Behind it a wall safe appeared.

It felt so creepy. "Skye, are you sure this is okay?" I whispered.

"Of course. Daddy keeps extra money in

the safe for emergencies. And my allowance definitely qualifies as an emergency." She smiled and I laughed, kind of nervously. "He wouldn't have given me the combination if I wasn't supposed to have it, would he?"

That made sense. What did I know about being rich? I had to promise Mom I would wash the car to get a measly five-dollar advance on my allowance.

Skye removed a money box from the safe and unlatched it. A mound of bills sprang free. She grabbed two twenties while my eyes danced with dollar signs.

We headed for the bus stop, joking around and giggling all the way. As we settled into the backseat of the bus, Skye asked who I liked. Under threat of torture if she so much as breathed a word, I finally told her: Daniel Oakes. "He's the absolute hottest guy I've ever seen," I said. "But I'm not going out with anyone." I added in a mutter, "Not since that rat Rob was bowed over by Tanya the mouse."

"Rob who?" she asked.

"Berkowitz. Do you know him?"

"Yeah, I think so. Curly hair and glasses?"

I nodded.

"He's in my history class," she said. "You must really like him."

"No, not like that. We're just friends."

"Come on, Kacie." She elbowed me.

"No, really, Skye."

"Uh-huh."

The bus squealed to a stop and I followed Skye up the aisle to the exit. As we stepped off, I asked her if she was going out with anyone. "No," she said. "I just broke up with my boyfriend over the summer." She took a deep breath and looked away.

That, along with the loss of her mother—I couldn't stand it. "Do you want to talk about it?"

"Not really. I'd rather hear about Vicky and Kyle," she said, as we entered the mall through some double glass doors.

"You mean that they went to a dance at the Razz together?"

"Everyone knows that. I mean about afterward. I saw Candace Torrey at the library this morning and—"

"What exactly did Candace Torrey say?" I demanded.

Skye leaned closer to me and spoke in a low voice. "She said Vicky and Kyle went to

Inspiration Point after their date."

I exploded. "That's not true! You know you can't believe a word Candace says. Vicky would never . . . I mean, she'd tell me first and . . . no, she wouldn't. I mean, she hasn't told me. I haven't talked to her, but I know it's not true. Look, Skye. Don't spread it around, okay? Vicky's not like that."

Skye shrugged. "Sure. Okay. I just thought you'd know since you're her best friend. I figured she'd call you first and fill you in on all the details. Candace said she saw her, but maybe it was someone else. Someone who just looked like Vicky."

We stepped onto the escalator together. My mind was racing. It seemed that Vicky had more important things to do than call her best friend after her biggest date ever. What *did* happen? Did she and Kyle actually go to Inspiration Point? Would she? Of course not! Never in a million years. What was I thinking? I'd call her as soon as I got home. She'd die. She'd absolutely die. This was a vicious rumor, a damaging one, and the sooner I put the skids to it the better.

Nine

SKYE and I hauled the mall for hours. We chose our future prom dresses and modeled feathered hats, tried on gloves, giggled over the funny cards in the gift shop, and cuddled the stuffed animals. I hadn't had so much fun since . . . well, since the last time Vicky and I'd gone to the mall. Which was ages ago.

I was conducting a scientific experiment, spraying an exotic-smelling perfume on Skye's neck to see how exotic she'd become, when the glowing digits on my watch caught my eye.

"Yikes! Skye, it's almost five o'clock! We'd better get going. Your dad's going to have a cow."

She shrugged. "We don't have to go. I hate those stupid dinners and Daddy knows it. He'll go without me if I'm not there."

"Don't you think you should at least call? I mean, he doesn't even know where you are. Won't he be worried?"

She laughed. "Daddy? Worried about me? Come on, Kacie. Let's check out the music store. I'm dying for the new Teal Duk tape."

"I don't know, Skye. I think we should call . . ." My words were lost in a trail of perfume as Skye took off. I hurried to catch up.

In the music store, we wandered around for a few minutes until I began to feel nervous about the time again. "Skye, I really think we should go," I said. "Even if your dad's okay about this, my parents are probably getting worried about me. Don't forget—we left my dad with the impression you guys would be dropping me off around now. Maybe I should call home." I glanced uneasily at my watch.

"Just one more minute," said Skye. "Let me look for this other tape." She headed toward the back of the store while I paced anxiously in the rock records section up front. Suddenly, she caught my elbow from behind. "Okay, let's go, Kacie. We can catch the next bus if we hurry." Skye raced ahead of me, and I scrambled to catch up.

We arrived at the bus stop just as a bus was pulling away. Skye flagged it down with a wave, and we hopped on board.

"I had a super time today," she said, flopping into the backseat. "You're so fun to be with, and, well . . . I've never been very good at expressing my feelings, so here." She dumped three cassettes in my lap.

"Skye, no! Don't buy me stuff! You don't have to. I know how you feel." I paused for a moment to stare at the tapes. "Which ones did you get?"

She laughed. "Your favorites, of course. It's no big deal, Kacie. I like giving you things. I'm really glad we're friends."

It was weird. I'd never known anyone as generous as Skye. Okay, I'd never known anyone as *rich* as Skye. I couldn't believe it. The new Jon Alys album. XLR8 and Teal Duk. Together, in one lap.

The bus dropped us off at the gate and we hustled toward Skye's house, giggling and chattering all the way. When we stumbled in the front door, Mr. Collinsworth was there, in the foyer, all dressed up. His jaw seemed like it was set in cement.

"Where have you been?" he demanded. His voice fairly boomed off the walls. "It's past six. The Baxters have been calling for almost an hour, wondering where we are. I thought I told you to stay home, Skye."

"See? I told you," she snarled at me. "Oh, Daddy. I'm so sorry." She hung her head.

You told me what? I wondered in shock.

Her father narrowed his eyes. "I believe you owe me an explanation, Skye."

"Of course." She looked straight at me and said, "Kacie got tired of studying and talked me into going to the mall."

I just about hyperventilated, right there in the foyer.

Skye gazed apologetically at her father. "She just wanted to buy a tape, so I didn't think it would take very long. I thought we'd be back in plenty of time for me to get ready. But Kacie wanted to try some perfume, then look at jewelry. The time just slipped away. I'm sorry, Daddy. Please don't be angry."

Mr. Collinsworth's dark eyes locked onto me. My chin hit the floor, I'm sure. I don't know if I was trembling more from fear or anger.

"Is that true, Kacie?" he asked.

Skye bit her lip. Her eyes pleaded with me. I didn't know what to say. I wasn't sure I could remember how to speak.

"Well?" Mr. Collinsworth demanded.

Geez! "Well, I did want to go to the mall," I said. "I'm sorry we were so late. We should have called so you wouldn't be worried." My eyes bored through the leather of his wingtip shoes.

"Worry is only one of my concerns," he said. "Baxter's support is vital if I'm going to gain the backing necessary to push through the new school mill levy. Do you understand?"

I nodded, because even though I didn't know what he was talking about, I did understand one thing: He was furious. And he didn't seem as concerned about what might have happened to Skye as he was about a stupid dinner party.

"I wanted to call you, Daddy, but Kacie kept promising we wouldn't be much longer," said Skye.

I threatened her with eye daggers.

Mr. Collinsworth ordered Skye upstairs to get ready, and me into the car. Oh, great. He was still going to drive me home.

We didn't say one word during the entire trip. I wanted to tell him the truth but every time I opened my mouth to speak he set his jaw harder. I didn't want him to break a tooth on my account.

When we arrived at my house I literally leaped from the Mercedes and raced inside. Dad was slumped in his easy chair, nodding off to a college football game. "Hi, Dad," I said with a sigh, plopping onto the couch.

"About time you got back," he said. "Did you have a good time?"

"Oh, yeah. Terrific. If you like hanging on a bloody meat hook after the slaughter."

He gave me a puzzled look, then said, "You know, Kacie, I figured you would be home at least an hour ago. Your mom and I were getting worried. Why didn't you call?"

"I wanted to, but Skye wouldn't let me."

He arched an eyebrow.

"Dad, she dragged me to the mall and wouldn't leave. I wanted to call. I tried to, but . . ." This sounded familiar. Too familiar. And just as lame the second time around.

"But what?" he asked. "She had you bound and gagged?"

I shook my head. "No. I could have found a way to call. I'm sorry. It won't happen again."

"Good." Dad sat up and stretched. "Oh, by the way, Vicky called. I told her you were at Skye's and should be home around five. She didn't leave a message—"

"Dad! You didn't! How could you?" I bolted from the couch. Right before I slammed my bedroom door, I heard Dad yell, "Hey, what did I do?"

Vicky wasn't home, naturally, but as soon as I hung up, the phone rang. It was Skye.

"Dad just got back from dropping you off and we'll be leaving for that boring dinner in a second, so I can't talk long," she whispered. "But I wanted to say thanks for lying for me, Kacie."

"I didn't lie. And you're not welcome. You lied to *me*, Skye. You said your father wouldn't mind. You said he would go to the dinner without you. Why didn't you just tell him the truth?"

"You *know* why. Any little thing sets him

off. You saw how mad he was. I knew he wouldn't yell at you, though. Oops, here he comes. Talk to you later." She paused. "Kacie? You're the best friend I've ever had. And I'm going to prove it."

Ten

F OR the entire next week, my head was spinning so much that I just sort of put my life on hold. I was so mixed up. Skye baffled me. I liked her; I wanted us to be friends. But after her little stunt in front of her father, I wasn't sure I could trust her again. On the other hand, I guess I couldn't blame her. I might have reacted the same way if my father acted as cold as Mr. Collinsworth. And Skye *did* call almost immediately afterward to apologize.

I lifted the turquoise scarf from the corner of my dresser mirror and absentmindedly trailed it through my fingers, letting my thoughts wander. Vicky was obviously too busy to include me in her life anymore. A whole week had passed and she *still* hadn't even told me about her date. I considered myself lucky if I spotted her in the hall long enough to wave.

How long had it been since we had talked, *really* talked? I needed her. When you need your best friend, you need her now, not tomorrow or next week, or whenever she can pencil you in on her busy calendar.

Maybe I'll call Rob, I thought, starting to pick up the phone. No, I decided against it. He was so wrapped up in Tanya lately that he was barely even saying "hi" to me in the halls. His eyes were permanently glazed over. We used to talk every day, but Rob hadn't spoken to me since . . . since when? The Dairy Kreme. I only vaguely remembered the last time he told me I was outstanding.

My mind drifted back to Skye. I had pretty much steered clear of her for the week. I hated knowing she was a cheater, and now a liar, too. But deep down, she wasn't a bad person. I believed that. She had some serious problems, and she was making bad choices at the moment. But maybe, if I was a good enough friend, I could help her change.

"I wish she'd stop giving me presents, though," I said out loud, staring at the stack of tapes by my stereo. I still felt strange about accepting them. Almost ashamed. Was Skye trying to buy my friendship, like Dad had said?

Then another thought hit me—I envied her. Actually, it wasn't her I envied so much as all the expensive things she had. Why would she want to hang around with me? I almost felt privileged she'd even consider me for a friend.

My eyes scanned the desk top where my jewelry box lay open. The gold chain twinkled under the desk lamp. I pulled the silk scarf through my fingers once more as I focused again on the stack of tapes. Something wasn't right. I was disturbed about all this. I just couldn't put my finger on exactly what was bothering me. If only I could talk to Vicky about it. If only . . .

Suddenly determined, I reached for the phone and punched in Vicky's number.

"She's meeting with a couple of kids involved in that Fun Committee, Kacie,"

Mrs. Anselli informed me. "I'll have her call you when she gets home."

"Never mind," I mumbled and hung up. Under my breath I added, "I wouldn't want to take up any of her precious time."

* * * * *

By Saturday night, I couldn't sleep at all. I tossed and turned for hours, my mind playing out scenes with Skye and Vicky. I was so angry with Vicky, and so confused about Skye. Would I be better off without them? No. It was hard enough to find someone—*anyone*—to really relate to. And truthfully, I was getting lonely. For my own peace of mind though, I needed to give the presents back to Skye. Avoiding her wasn't the way to go. But I didn't want our friendship based on my envy, gratitude, or greed—or whatever it was I was feeling.

I threw back the covers and rolled out of bed. In the hall closet I found a box just the right size. I tossed in all the gifts from Skye, sealed the box with masking tape, and shoved it in the back of my closet. On Monday it was all going back.

With that resolved, I could finally sleep.

* * * * *

In the morning, the phone jangled next to my ear, jarring me from sleep.

"Hello," I said in a foggy voice.

"It's me."

"Hi, Rob," I said, brightening. "So you *do* remember your social savior." I propped up against my pillow. "What's up?"

"Did you talk to Tanya this week?" he asked.

I wrinkled my nose. "Talk to her about what? You? How boring. Or maybe you think we had a deep discussion about Tchaikovsky's Symphony in B-Plus Majorly F-Flats."

I giggled. He didn't, though, and I sat up straighter.

"Do you know anyone who would have talked to her?" Rob continued. "About me and . . . and you?"

"Why? What's going on? What happened?"

There was an uncomfortable pause. "Tanya doesn't want to see me anymore. All I know is that it has something to do with you. What did you say to her, Kacie?"

"Nothing! I swear. I haven't talked to her. I don't think I've talked to anyone but myself all week long!"

Rob totally ignored what I was saying. "It's obvious you don't like her," he continued, "but I didn't think you'd go this far. Is this what you meant at Dairy Kreme when you threatened to 'get me'?"

"What do you mean? I didn't . . . I didn't do anything!" I was almost speechless. "Rob, give me Tanya's number. I'll call her and see if I can find out—"

"Not a chance. You've already done enough damage. Just leave her alone. Okay?" He hung up.

I felt my face heat to red. Rob had never talked to me like that before. He was really upset. His voice was even shaking. Before I could talk myself out of it, I called the information operator and got Tanya's number. Then I tapped in the digits.

"Hello?" a weak voice answered.

"Tanya?"

"Yes." In the background I could hear her blow her nose.

"This is Kacie. Kacie Shannon? I just talked to Rob. I'm trying to find out what happened this week."

"As if you don't know," she said cooly. I wanted to scream.

"I *don't* know. Tell me. He said it had something to do with me."

"Why don't you ask Candace Torrey?"

"Candace? Did she tell you something about me and Rob? Is she spreading lies?"

The phone clicked in my hand. Geez, what was this all about? I called Vicky. For once, she was there. I didn't waste any time getting right to the point.

"Vicky, Rob called and he's all upset. Something happened between him and Tanya and it has to do with me. She basically told him to get out of her life. I called her to find out what was going on and she said Candace Torrey—"

"Don't mention that name to me, Kacie," said Vicky. "Do you know what she's telling everyone about me and Kyle? I'm so embarrassed. He won't even look at me in the hall anymore. And I don't blame him. Did you say something to her about us?"

I almost swallowed the phone. "Me?"

"Well, as far as I know, you're the only one who knew he was taking me out. I didn't tell anyone else. Listen, I have to go. We're going to my grandparents' house for lunch." The receiver buzzed in my ear.

I just lay there in bed clutching the dead phone. What was going on? What was happening to me and my friends? My whole world was falling apart. Everyone I cared about was hurt or mad and somehow, it seemed to be all my fault. I stared at the phone in my hand for the longest time until finally, I couldn't stand it anymore. I threw it across the room.

Eleven

OVER the next several days I called Vicky and Rob every chance I got. Vicky was never home. Either she was cheerleading at a game or practicing for the play or at a Fun Committee meeting. Rob was always practicing too—or at least that was his excuse. If their strategy was to avoid me, they were following through perfectly.

It wasn't until late Wednesday that Vicky and I connected at all. I ran into her in the hall, but she was dashing off to Computer Tutor, some new service program at school, and she could only talk for a minute.

"Hey, how are you?" I asked, skip-hopping beside her down the hall.

"Fine. And you?"

This was my best friend? Chill out. "Fine. How are things between you and Kyle? He can't be mad about a stupid lie."

"Kyle and I are history, Kacie."

"You're kidding! Geez, I'm sorry, Vicky. Believe me, I didn't have anything to do with it." We paused at the main hall intersection.

"I don't have time to talk right now," she said, avoiding eye contact. "Can I call you later?" She didn't wait for my answer before hurrying off.

"When later?" I called to her back. "When you have time? Just when is that, Vicky? Sometime this year? In this lifetime? I thought we were friends. Best friends. But forget it. Just forget it. It's impossible to be friends with you. You don't have time, especially for a nobody like me!" I suddenly realized I was shouting at the top of my lungs in the crowded hallway.

Vicky stopped, turned slowly, and locked eyes with me. Then her face softened. Shaking her head, she walked back to me. "I'm sorry, Kace," she said. "I'm just really busy right now. It's not forever, I promise. As soon as things slow down with cheerleading, and once the Fun Committee finishes plans for the Christmas dance, and then when play rehearsals settle down . . ."

I just looked at her.

Vicky swallowed hard. "I promise I'll call you. Maybe we can get together after school. Oh wait, I have a game to cheer at. Sorry. What about this weekend? Can you sleep over on Friday?"

Immediately I brightened, then remembered that I couldn't. "Mom's birthday is Friday. We're all going out for dinner and a movie. Hey, do you want to come? You could sleep over afterward and we could catch up on things."

The bell rang and she began to walk backward. "Wait a minute. Friday's no good. I completely forgot. I'm going out, too. What about Saturday?"

"Who are you going out with?"

"Saturday?"

"No, Friday."

"Did I say I was going out? I meant I was going out for the drama club. I'm thinking of joining, since I made the play."

"Life isn't dramatic enough for you?"

"Huh?"

Geez, she didn't even laugh at my jokes

anymore. We didn't seem to communicate at all.

"Listen, I really have to run," said Vicky. "We'll work it out later, okay?" She turned on her heel and sprinted off, leaving me alone in the deserted hallway.

That night, as I was sticking pins into last year's school picture of Candace Torrey, the phone rang. I lunged to pick it up, hoping, praying it was Vicky.

"Hi, Kacie. What are you doing?"

At least it was a cheery voice. "Hi, Skye. Nothing much." Glancing toward my closet, I realized the box of presents was still in there. Naturally, I'd forgotten to give them back. Out of sight, out of mind.

"You've seemed so down for the last week and a half," she said. "Is anything wrong?"

"Wrong? You mean besides weeks and weeks of algebra yet?"

She laughed. I sighed. I didn't want to burden Skye with my problems. Besides, it was majorly uncool to put down one friend in front of another. "It's nothing, Skye. But thanks for caring."

"I do care. I've missed the old Kacie. We haven't passed secret notes for at least a week."

For a while we had been writing notes to each other, just to goad Oh Tannenbaum. The notes were stupid, juvenile, like:

"Are you still hot for R.B.?"

"I told you we were just friends."

"Oh, I forgot."

"Now D.O. He's hot!!! I've been in love with him since the first time I laid eyes on him in sixth grade."

"Why don't you call him?"

"I can't get up the nerve."

"Oh, sure. You? I think you're just waiting around for R.B. to drop T.M."

"WE ARE JUST FRIENDS!!!"

"Uh-huh. I heard a rumor that V.A. is going out with K.Z. True?"

"Yeah. They went out to the Razz last weekend. He is sooooo cool!!!"

"Tell me about it."

And so on—real kindergarten. But it was more fun than factoring equations off the board.

I juggled the phone to my other ear and sighed. I could hear music blasting from Skye's stereo in the background.

"I have an idea," said Skye. "Why don't

you come over, like maybe tomorrow after school? We could watch MTV or something. Or, if you insist, we could do homework."

I was about to say no, but I was restless and I needed to get my mind off Vicky. "I have a better idea. Why don't you come over here?" Immediately, I bit my tongue. It wasn't a better idea at all. I didn't want Skye to see my house. Compared to hers, it was a hovel.

Fortunately she said, "I can't. I'm grounded till Saturday. I'm not supposed to leave the house." She groaned. "Two more days of agony."

"What are you grounded for?"

Skye hesitated. "You remember. For coming home late from the mall that Saturday we went shopping?"

How could I forget? "Yeah, let's talk about that, Skye—"

She cut me short. "Let's not. It's history, and I already apologized. Can we just drop it? I . . . I just wasn't thinking straight. I mean, haven't you ever been so scared that you said something you didn't really mean, and it turned out to be a lie? You didn't really plan to lie—it just came out that way?"

Like when Dad asked why I didn't call?

"I guess I have," I admitted. "But I'm a terrible liar. I usually end up spilling my guts in about two minutes."

Skye laughed. "Yeah. Me, too."

She must have told her father the truth after all, I thought, feeling relieved.

"So will you come?" she pleaded. "I really have missed your warped sense of humor."

"On one condition, Skye. We study."

She groaned. "Okay."

"I mean it, Skye. I'm way behind. The algebra midterm is coming up and I haven't even started the chapter on distributive improbabilities, or whatever it is."

"I know. Me neither. Even with a weekend coming up, I'm not sure I'll make it. I am sure I'll never make it without your help."

I felt better all of a sudden. Skye had a knack for doing that.

* * * * *

The next day, I rode the bus home with Skye after school. In a deadpan voice she said she had been looking forward to studying all day. That cracked us both up. Her father was out campaigning again, so we played some music. We concluded that we needed something fun to get us in the mood for algebra. The hours drifted by. Finally, we ordered a pizza and ate in her bedroom.

After the pizza, we actually did open our algebra books—for about a microsecond. Skye asked how Rob was and I lost all interest in studying. I told her we were barely speaking. Then I filled her in on the Tanya incident.

"He really liked her," I said, shaking my head sadly. "I don't know what happened."

"Maybe it wasn't meant to be," Skye said, smiling slightly. She elbowed me. "You'll probably get him back now."

"Skye, I keep telling you that it's not like that between Rob and me. It never has been."

"Uh-huh."

She couldn't seem to get it through her head that Rob and I were just friends. It didn't matter, because the next thing Skye said blew the whole subject out of state.

"I've been thinking about getting back together with Kyle." She sprawled across the bed and hugged a pillow.

"Kyle who?" I asked.

"Kyle Zimmer. Didn't I tell you? He was my boyfriend last year."

My eyes must have popped out of their sockets. "You're kidding! You and Kyle?"

"We went together last semester." She pushed up to her feet, plowed across the floor to her vanity, and began to test lipstick. My mouth was stuck in the open position. "I'm sure I told you that," she said.

"No, Skye. I'm sure you didn't."

She shrugged. "Oh, well. I had to break up with him because he wanted to go too far. I wasn't ready." She tossed the lipstick into the trash before returning to the bed to sit next to me. "He called me for weeks, begging me not to break it off. I felt so awful." Skye's face sagged. "I still love him, Kacie. Sometimes I wonder if I did the right thing. I mean, maybe I'm just a prude."

"No," I said firmly. "You weren't just being a prude." Now I understood now why Skye was so hostile toward Vicky. It was horrible knowing that the person you loved was going out with someone else.

I put my hand on her shoulder. "It just takes time to heal, Skye. And you're not alone. Remember, you have me. Warp factor one?" I rapped the top of my head with a knuckle.

Skye laughed. "You're wacko, you know that?" She squeezed my hand. "You're also my best friend. The best friend I've ever had."

Was that true? I felt guilty because I didn't exactly feel the same way about her. Of course, right now she did seem to be my only friend.

A door closed downstairs and Skye jumped to her feet. "Daddy's home!" she cried, her eyes lighting up. "I can't believe it. He's never home this early. Let's go say 'hi.' Maybe he'll take us out for ice cream." She nearly wrenched my arm out of its socket as she yanked me toward the door.

Memories of my last encounter with Mr. Collinsworth still haunted me. I nervously glanced at my watch. "Geez, look at the time. I'd better get going."

Her face fell. "Do you have to?"

I nodded. "I really do. It's a school night. My curfew's eight-thirty." And, I suddenly remembered, Skye and I still hadn't done any algebra. I would have to work the whole weekend to finish all the problems.

I grabbed my coat and followed Skye downstairs. The door to Mr. Collinsworth's study was closed, but Skye just flung it open and waltzed in. "Hi, Daddy," she chirped, hugging him around the neck.

He loosened her grip and leaned closer to a tape player. From what I could make out, he was apparently listening to a speech from the guy running against him in the election. A deep voice rumbled out of the tape player: ". . . my worthy opponent, Congressman Collinsworth, voted twice last term to decrease the budget for highways. If I'm elected . . ."

"Will you take Kacie home?" Skye asked.

Mr. Collinsworth shushed her.

"Daddy!"

He punched the stop button and turned a frown on Skye. "I'm extremely busy, Skye. You know that. The debate is next weekend and I have a lot of research to do before then. I thought I asked you to stay out of the study when the door was closed. What do you want?"

When he noticed me, it was instant lockjaw.

"Will you take Kacie home?" Skye asked again.

"Come on, Skye." I tugged at her sleeve. "Your father's busy. I'll just call my dad."

She persisted, as if she hadn't heard me, "Well? Will you?"

Mr. Collinsworth sighed wearily. I knew that sigh. It meant, "I'd rather eat slugs."

I quickly volunteered, "That's okay, Mr. Collinsworth. I can call my dad."

"Fine," he mumbled. He turned back to the recording.

"Daddy!" Skye wailed.

He didn't even flinch.

I grabbed her arm and backed toward the door. In a whisper I said, "It's okay, Skye. My dad doesn't mind. Really."

She looked at me for an instant, then burst into tears. Fleeing from the room, she left me alone in the study with Mad Dog Collinsworth. He glanced up momentarily to snarl at me. Unexpectedly, he opened a drawer in his desk. The vision of a loaded revolver flashed in my mind. I raced from the room, down the hall, and out the front door. And I didn't stop running until I reached my front door at home.

Twelve

I flew in the house at exactly nine-fifteen. I know because I had been eyeing my watch for the last mile or so, willing it to stop ticking. Mom and Dad were waiting for me, as I knew they would be. Mom had her hands on her hips. Dad had a major scowl on his face.

"Sorry I'm late," I wheezed. "I didn't have any money for the bus. And I couldn't call." I bent over to catch my breath. "I ran as fast as I could. But you know how far it is to Skye's. I'm sorry."

"You *ran* home from Skye's house?" Dad yelled. "At night?"

"What on earth were you thinking?" Mom pitched in.

"Don't you *ever* do that again, do you understand?" Dad was riled. "You call us, Kacie. No matter what, you find a way to call." He paused, and inhaled deeply. "Maybe you ought to just stay home from now on. That way curfew won't be such a problem."

I straightened up and gulped. "Are you saying I'm grounded?"

Mom and Dad gave each other one of those looks filled with all sorts of nonverbal codes that parents communicate with. Then Mom grumbled something, turned and stalked away. Dad lectured me for another five minutes, but never actually said I was grounded. I took this to mean I was getting a reprieve—this time—and I slinked off to my room.

I should have been mad at Skye. Obviously, she hadn't told her father the truth, since he still despised me. But after the way he tossed her aside tonight, I felt more embarrassed for her than anything.

The next day, Skye barely looked at me in class. And when the bell rang, she tore off before I could talk to her. Vicky was nowhere to be found, and Rob made a wide arc in the hall past me, as if I were an alien from the Planet Leprosy.

Even Mom's birthday party that night was depressing. Because she was turning forty this year, Dad and I had decorated the car with black balloons that said "Over the Hill." Great idea. Mom burst into tears when she saw it.

Saturday morning, I telephoned Vicky on a whim. She wasn't home. By now I expected that, but when Mrs. Anselli informed me Vicky had taken a weekend babysitting job for the Harrelsons, an arrow pierced my heart.

The Harrelsons were an older couple who went to Florida every year for some senior citizens' convention. They always called us to babysit. Vicky and I had made a fortune over the years watching their dog, Baby. We had a long-standing agreement that we would always babysit for the Harrelsons together, and pool the money for Paris.

Vicky hadn't even called me to tell me they were going. Maybe she didn't want to share the money anymore. Maybe she didn't want to share *anything* anymore.

Strictly out of habit I called Rob. He was

practicing. Practicing avoiding me.

I felt a hot tear roll down my cheek. Then another on the other side. Suddenly the floodgates just burst apart, and I buried my face in my pillow to muffle the sobs.

I must have cried for an hour. In all that time, no one called. No one cared. When no more tears would come, I sat up and blew my nose. Finally, there was only one thing left to do—algebra. With a sigh of resignation, I settled at my desk, popped on my earphones, and opened my algebra book. I knew it was hopeless, though. Without Vicky's help I would never be able to do the problems. Say hello to an *F* and goodbye to my allowance forever.

After what seemed like an eternity, I had completed all the practice problems on the handouts. And when I checked the answers, I found I had only missed two. I was kind of proud of myself—amazed, actually—that I could do this well on my own.

As I was cutting myself a congratulatory slice of chocolate cake, the phone rang.

"Kacie, hi!" said Skye. "I've been working on algebra all morning, and if I don't quit soon I'm going to go stark raving mad. Do you want to come over? Daddy's gone and we can play tapes all afternoon. Or study, if you'd rather do that. Please say you wouldn't."

I laughed. I had two more chapters in algebra to read, but at the rate I was going, I felt confident I could finish them by tomorrow night, easy. And it was so good to hear a friendly voice. "Maybe I will come over, Skye. I could use a break myself."

"Great! I'll warm up the stereo. Hurry, I'm starting to feel faint. This is it. I'm going, going, gahhh . . ."

I giggled as the phone hit the floor. After I hung up—and after a brief lecture from Mom about responsibility—I snagged a bus. About twenty minutes later I arrived on Skye's doorstep.

"I have a super idea," she said, ushering me up the stairs. "Let's call Kyle Zimmer."

I widened my eyes at her. "Why?"

"You know. To see if he still feels the same way about me. I've decided I want us to get back together." Skye lifted her hair up over her shoulders and flopped down on the bed.

I frowned. "Does that mean you've

changed your mind about . . ." I trailed off.

She gazed into her full-length mirror. "I still love him, you know. If I could just talk to him, tell him how I feel, I think we could work it out. I think he'd be willing to wait."

Boy, love really is blind. I shrugged. "All right. Go ahead and call."

She batted her eyelashes at me. "Not me. You."

"Me? Why me? I don't even know him."

"Sure you do." She pulled me down next to her. "He went out with your best friend, didn't he?"

"What does that have to do with anything? Skye, he doesn't know me from—"

"Please, Kacie?" she pleaded. "Be a friend and do this for me?" As she was talking, she was punching in the numbers on her phone. Then she handed me the receiver.

Somebody answered. "Hello?"

Rotten luck. He was home. "Uh, hello. Is this Kyle?"

"Yeah. Who's this?"

"You don't know me. I mean, we met once. Sort of. At the Dairy Kreme? You were sitting in my booth. With Vicky. Vicky Anselli?" Geez, I felt like an idiot.

110

Kyle said, "Try me again. What's your name?"

Yeah, my name. "Kacie Shannon."

"Oh, right. Vicky's friend. Hi, Kacie. Hey, why is she mad at me, anyway? What did I do? She won't even talk to me at school."

"Mad at you? I thought you were mad—"

Skye nudged me. She stood up and leaned against the bureau, arms folded. "Uh, the reason I'm calling, Kyle . . ." What was I going to say? I cleared my throat and started again. "Do you remember Skye Collinsworth?" Stupid, of course he did. They were extremely in love, weren't they?

"Yeeeah," he answered slowly.

I could see he wasn't going to make this easy. "Well, she's a friend of mine."

"That's too bad," he muttered.

"What?"

"Nothing."

I smiled at Skye and took a deep breath. "I was wondering how you felt about her. If she was, you know, willing to go out with you again, would you be interested?"

Kyle snorted. "Willing to go out with me?" There was a long pause. "Kacie, you tell Skye I meant what I said to her. Tell her my feelings haven't changed."

I covered the phone. In an excited whisper I relayed the message. "He says his feelings haven't changed!"

Skye smiled faintly.

"Tell her I think she's a psycho," Kyle said in my ear. "I'll never go out with her again. It took me months to get her off my back. Did she tell you she used to call me every night? When I refused to talk to her, she'd call every ten minutes and hang up. It went on all summer. My parents were ready to kill me."

My cheeks must have flushed as pink as Skye's sweater. She paced nervously in front of me. "Come on, Kyle," I said. "You're not being fair. How do you know it was her?"

He dropped the subject. "Look, the next time you talk to Vicky, will you ask her what happened between us? I can never get in touch with her. I really want to know why she's mad."

"Yeah, sure." I didn't tell him he might have a long wait before Vicky and I ever talked again.

We hung up. I handed the phone to Skye and she hung it up.

"Well?" she demanded.

I breathed deeply, then again. Maybe this was one of those rare instances when lying was justified. At least it would spare her feelings. "Kyle said that, uh, since you dropped him he was . . . uh, going out with someone else right now. That's it. He's kind of, uh, in a relationship. He said he doesn't want to go out with you. I mean, he *can't*. He won't. He . . ." I trailed off, lost in my own maze of deception.

"Doesn't want to go out with me?" Skye repeated. "Is that what he said? I don't believe you, Kacie. Don't look at me like that. I'm the one who broke it off. I am!" She whirled and stomped across the room. "You're lying, Kacie. I don't know why, but you're just trying to hurt me. And after all I did for you and Rob."

"That's not true. Skye! I would never hurt—" I stopped short. "Wait a minute. What did you do for me and Rob?"

She turned and glared at me. "I got rid of Tanya."

My mouth flopped open. "Skye, what did you do? What *exactly* did you do?"

Skye flipped her hair over her shoulder. "I know you like Rob. So I made up a little note to Tanya." She rummaged around on the top of her vanity. "Here's a copy of it. All it took was some creative cut and paste, plus Daddy's state-of-the-art photo copier in the study. Here." She thrust the note at me.

I thought I was going to be sick. Skye had saved all the stupid notes we had passed in algebra. Then she had cut up the messages in my handwriting, carefully reassembled them, and made a photo copy that looked incredibly like a real letter. It read: "R.B. . . . is the hottest guy in school. I've been in love with him since the first time I laid eyes on him in sixth grade . . . He finally got up the nerve to . . . ask . . . me . . . out to the Razz last weekend."

It went on sickeningly until the end, where my bold signature nearly burned my fingers through the page.

"You gave this to Tanya?" I asked weakly. Skye smiled. "Not me, actually. I asked Candace Torrey to deliver it during orchestra. She's a perfect scapegoat, don't you think?" Skye laughed.

I was fuming. "How *could* you? I told you Rob and I were just friends. I never wanted to break him and Tanya up! This must have really hurt her feelings, not to mention what it did to Rob. No wonder he's avoiding me like the plague!"

"You're such a liar, Kacie," Skye said. "You can't be just friends with a guy. Even I know that. You were just using friendship as an excuse to be with him all the time."

I jumped to my feet, clenching my fists. "Quit it, Skye! Just quit it. You're wrong. You're wrong about me and Rob." The chill in my voice froze Skye in place. For a moment we stared intensely at each other. Then Skye abruptly burst into tears.

I took a deep breath. What a mess. What was I going to do? I had to think this through, and Skye's wailing wasn't helping me concentrate.

"Look, Skye," I said, feeling myself backing down, "I know you were only trying to help, but geez. Now I know why Rob hates my guts, and I don't blame him."

Skye bit her trembling lip. "I thought I was doing you a favor, as a friend, which is a lot more than I can say for you." She sniffled.

"What do you mean?"

She looked at me. "You sure didn't try very hard with Kyle on the phone just now."

I had no idea what to say. "I'm sorry about Kyle. I did ask him. What did you want me to do? Beg?"

"If that's what it takes."

Did she mean that? Didn't she have any self-respect? We stared at each other again. Then Skye lowered her head and said, "I don't want to fight with you, Kacie. You're the only friend I have. I'm sorry about Rob. I thought I was doing something nice, but I always mess everything up." She grabbed a Kleenex and blew her nose.

All I could do was shake my head.

"Let's get out of here for a while," she said, forcing a shaky smile. "I know—let's go to the mall. There's a new tape out that I've been dying to get for you."

Thirteen

I didn't want to go to the mall with Skye, but that didn't matter. Whatever Skye wanted, Skye got. I suppose I could have said no, but she would have talked me into it. Why did we always end up doing what she wanted? Because I was a pushover, a fourteen-year-old bowl of Jell-O.

We caught the bus and arrived at the mall a little after one. Skye had brightened considerably by then, acting as if nothing had happened. I couldn't switch moods that fast. I felt sort of bruised, inside and out.

"Ooh, look, there's a sale on sweaters," Skye chirped, pointing to a second-floor clothing store as we rode the up escalator. "I also saw an ad in the paper for a half-price sale on gold chains at the jewelry store. "Oh, gross. Look." She pointed to the mezzanine below. "There's Candace Torrey."

My eyes followed Skye's finger. "No doubt picking up trash for next week's dumping," I muttered as we stepped off the escalator.

Skye said, "We used to be best friends, you know, until I heard that Kyle asked her out last summer. She still thinks I like her."

It didn't register, what she had just said. My own thoughts were crowding my mind. "Skye, I'll be back. I need to talk to Candace."

"No, don't," Skye said, but I was already on my way down the escalator, determined to confront "the mouth."

"Candace." I touched her shoulder and she whirled around. "That vicious rumor you're spreading about Vicky Anselli and Kyle Zimmer? I wish you'd quit it. It stinks, you know?"

"What rumor?" Candace asked, looping a piece of hair behind her ear. "I didn't say anything about them. Why would I? Kyle's my friend."

I flinched. "Someone told me you said—"

"Why does everyone think I'm spreading

all these rumors?" Like mercury in a thermometer, blood rushed up Candace's neck. "This has been going on for weeks now! I don't understand it. I never said anything. And I didn't start the one about Tara and Cameron either. Someone's out to get me. I wish I knew who hated me so much they would totally destroy my reputation." Her voice broke. All at once she burst into tears and raced past me.

Everything clicked then. My eyes drifted up to where Skye was leaning over the railing in front of the music store, looking down at me.

"Kacie, come on," she called. "I want to get in on the sales before all the good stuff is gone."

I realized now who had started the rumor about Vicky and Kyle. Skye hadn't stopped with just that note to Tanya . . . geez! She hurt people. She hurt people on purpose.

I caught the up escalator. Skye was impatiently waiting. "Come on, Kacie. We're going to miss out on everything if we don't hurry."

Mustering strength, I said, "Skye, I have to talk to you."

"Later, later," she replied, grabbing my sleeve and tugging me toward the store.

"Not later, and forget the stupid sale," I said. I jerked away from her.

Skye frowned. "What did Candace tell you anyway? You know you can't believe a word she says. She's such a liar. Now, come *on*, Kacie. We rode the bus all the way here. At least we should shop for a while." She held up her right hand. "I promise I won't buy you a present. Cross my heart and hope to die." She drew a cross against her heart with a finger.

I flopped down on a wooden bench. "Sit down, Skye," I ordered. "I have to talk to you." I gestured to the spot next to me.

She clucked, like it was a big imposition. Then she stalked off into the music store.

I hesitated for a minute, then shook my head, stood up, and followed her. She was browsing the tapes as I approached. "Skye, did you start the rumor about Vicky and Kyle?" I asked.

She pivoted toward me. "Is that what Candace told you? Oh, thanks a lot. You must really trust me." She turned back around.

I don't, I thought. I almost said so, too. "Look, Candace didn't tell me anything. I just figured it out. You did it all, didn't you, Skye? Rob and Tanya, Kyle and Vicky. Candace, too. You started all the rumors."

"So what?" said Skye without looking at me.

"So you hurt them."

She shrugged and picked up a cassette, pretending to read the label. "Everybody hurts, okay? It's a fact of life."

"Skye," I said, putting a hand on her shoulder, "I know you've had a rough time, what with your mom dying and all, but you can't just go off on people like that. I really think you should apologize."

Skye looked at me then. She glared. "Apologize? Forget it."

"Come on, Skye. You have to make things right. You're the only one who can do it."

"No way."

I swallowed hard. "Then I don't think we can be friends anymore."

Skye did a weird thing. She started to laugh, kind of hysterically. Then she tossed the cassette into her bag and marched out of the store. Only this time I didn't follow.

* * * * *

It wasn't until the next morning that it hit me, like a slap in the face. I was lying in bed replaying yesterday's events when I suddenly realized Skye had walked out of the music store without paying for the tape. What else had she stolen? I wondered. Probably her whole music collection.

Instinctively, I reached for the phone. I really needed Vicky's help now. Everything was a complete disaster. I couldn't begin to straighten it all out by myself. Rob and Tanya, Vicky and Kyle, Candace. What was I going to do about them? And Skye? How was I going to stop her?

As I began to punch in Vicky's phone number, I prayed, "Please be there, Vicky, pleeeease."

With my finger poised over the last digit of her phone number, I had a revelation. I didn't need Vicky to tell me what to do. This was *my* problem—my mess, my life. I'd gotten myself into trouble, and I had to get myself out. I set the receiver back into the cradle.

In the shower I figured out what I was going to do. First, I called Tanya. She hung up on me five times, but I kept calling back, explaining a little more each time until the whole rotten scheme was out in the open. When I finally stopped babbling, and didn't hear the buzz of a dead phone in my ear, I said, "Tanya, are you there?"

"Yes," she said quietly. "Is all of this true? You never wrote that note?"

"No, I didn't. I'm so sorry. I know it hurt your feelings, and Rob's, too. But believe me. Rob and I are just friends. I don't feel anything but friendship for him, I swear."

Tanya said, "He kept telling me that. I guess I just found it hard to believe. I've always been so jealous of you."

"Me?" My voice came out in a squeak. "You're jealous of *me*? Why? Oh, I know. My incredible singing voice." That cracked her up. "Listen, Tanya. Rob really likes you. I know he does. I'm going to call him right now and explain everything."

"No, Kacie. Let me," she said.

"Are you sure?"

"Yes. I need to hear his voice. I miss him so much."

She really was sweet.

"You know what?" she said. "You're a good friend to Rob. I hope the two of us . . ." Her voice trailed off.

"Me, too. And if Rob ever gives you any trouble, just let me know. I've got a lot of dirt on that guy."

Tanya laughed.

After we hung up, I took a deep breath. I felt better about Tanya, although I wasn't sure if I could ever get Rob to talk to me again. But there wasn't time to dwell on that right now. I had another call to make, this one to Kyle. He answered on the sixth ring, and unlike the last time, he remembered me right away.

"Hey, Kacie, did you ever talk to Vicky about me?"

Nothing like getting right down to it, I thought. "Yeah, I did, Kyle," I answered. "She isn't mad. It was all a stupid lie. A rumor. You see, Skye Collinsworth—"

He groaned.

"Don't worry. I'm not calling for her." I went on to explain how Skye had started a rumor about Inspiration Point and then blamed Candace.

"Oh, brother," Kyle said. "That sounds like something she'd dream up."

"Vicky didn't want to risk your reputation—or hers. She was so embarrassed."

Kyle groaned again.

"Anyway, I feel responsible. I hope the two of you can work it out."

"Me, too," he said. "Thanks for getting to the bottom of it, Kacie. I'll call Vicky right now. And Candace, too."

I heaved an enormous sigh of relief and wiped the palms of my hands on my jeans. I felt like the thick fog that had settled over me was finally lifting, slowly but surely. Two down. Clear Skye ahead.

Buried under a heap of clothes in my closet was the box of gifts from Skye. Fate must have been what kept me from returning them. I ripped the tape off the box and flung open the top. How could I have been so stupid? I knew now that every one of those presents had probably been stolen.

I just couldn't understand why. Why did Skye have to steal? She had enough money to buy everything she ever wanted. But confronting her with my suspicions wasn't going to change anything. She'd just lie. I didn't know what to do. I needed some expert advice on this one.

Dad was sitting at the table eating a bowl of cereal when I walked in. "Hi, Dad," I said. "Where's Mom?"

He looked up from the paperback he was reading. "She had her real estate class this morning." He glanced at the kitchen clock. "She should be back in an hour or so. We're out of milk, but I'll burn some toast for you if you're hungry." Dad burns everything he cooks. He grinned at his little joke, then slurped in a spoonful of cereal.

"No, thanks." I slumped into the chair opposite him.

He swallowed, then dog-eared the page of his book and set it down. "Uh-oh. You're not even cracking a smile. Anything your old dad can do to help?"

Dad was so cool. I inhaled deeply. "Please, Dad," I began. "Don't say 'I told you so.'"

He arched an eyebrow.

I told him the whole story about Skye,

and her cheating and lying, and finally what I suspected about her stealing. "Why would she do it, Dad? Steal, I mean. Her father's always giving her money."

"Hmm." Dad shoved his cereal bowl aside and leaned forward on his elbows. "Maybe money isn't what she really needs. You said her father isn't around much. Could it be Skye's just trying to get his attention? Maybe she *wants* to get caught."

I hadn't thought of that. It seemed like a desperate move, but maybe Skye had reached that point.

We sat there for a while in silence. The more I considered it, the more I was convinced Dad was right. Not only was Skye craving her father's attention; she was crying out for *anyone's* attention—anyone at all.

I thought out loud, "But how is she going to get her father's attention if he doesn't even know about all the stuff that's going on?"

"Hmm," Dad said again.

A scary thought flickered through my brain. "Someone has to tell him?" I raised questioning eyes to Dad.

He reached across the table and took my hand. "Do you want me to do it? I really should call Charles anyway and invite him over for dinner."

"No." I shook my head. "I have to do this. It's my responsibility. I just hope it doesn't ruin your friendship with him."

Dad gave a short laugh. "To tell you the truth, we never were that close. I always thought he was kind of a class-conscious snob." He shook his head. "We were never what I'd consider friends."

Fourteen

RATHER than have Dad drive me, I decided to take the bus to Skye's. The ride would give me time to rehearse what I was going to say.

I could have practiced for a year and it wouldn't have mattered. When Mr. Collinsworth answered the door, I froze.

"Was Skye expecting you?" he asked. "She's not here."

I gulped. No words came.

"I think she's at the library studying." He scratched his head. "Or was that yesterday?"

I swallowed again. "Actually, I came to see you," I said weakly.

His eyes narrowed. "What about?"

I just stood in the doorway, shivering. Make that trembling.

"Well, come in," he said at last. "I hope this won't take long. I have a mountain of paperwork to catch up on."

It won't if I can put together a single sentence, I thought. I followed him into his study.

"Please, sit down." Mr. Collinsworth pointed to a leather armchair and quietly closed the door. Then he sat down at his desk.

I tried to smile. This was harder than I ever imagined. *Get a grip, Kacie,* I commanded myself. I tightened my fingers on the armchair. "Mr. Collinsworth, I need to talk to you about Skye."

"Oh? What about her?"

Well, that answered my first question. She hadn't made a full confession to him overnight. I decided to blunder straight ahead and said, "Skye is a cheater, a liar, and a thief." Then I cringed.

Mr. Collinsworth cleared his throat. "What are you talking about?" he asked sternly.

"Yesterday at the mall I saw Skye steal a

tape. And that isn't all."

Expressionless, Mr. Collinsworth said, "Go on."

I made myself look directly at him. As if I were reading from a grocery list, I checked off each incident from the last several weeks, from cheating on the algebra test to the gifts Skye had given me to the rumors she had spread.

Her father didn't say a word. He just stared at me. Or through me. I couldn't read the look in his eyes at all. I figured if he was going to go for the revolver, this would be a good time. When he didn't make a move, I decided to press my luck.

I stood up and emptied the box of gifts over his desk. "I'm returning all the things Skye ever gave me just in case—well, you know."

Briefly, he scanned the articles. I saw his jaw tighten.

"She took money out of the safe, too," I said.

"She what?" Mr. Collinsworth's tone made the hairs on my neck stand up. Then he shot to his feet. My eyes followed him across the room to the wall safe. A minute later he returned to the desk with the money box, set it down, and flipped open the lid.

He removed all the money and counted it. Then his face turned pale. Up until then I don't think he believed me.

"How did she get the combination?" he asked.

"She said you gave it to her in case she ever needed money for emergencies."

He shook his head. "I didn't know she even knew about the wall safe." He blinked. "I guess there are a lot of things I don't know about Skye."

Mr. Collinsworth sank back into his chair and wheeled around, turning his back to me. That was definitely my cue to leave. I got up and tiptoed toward the door.

"Kacie?"

I turned to meet his eyes. "Thank you for coming to me with this. It . . . it took a lot of courage." He paused. "This isn't the first time Skye's been in trouble. Last year after the, uh, accident, there were some incidents at school. I thought maybe a transfer . . . a new start . . ."

He stared past me and didn't say anything for a few seconds. "Well, you have to understand," he said at last, "it's been extremely difficult for me, for us, ever since Mary's—Skye's mother's—death." His eyes met mine for a second, then lowered to his hands clasped in his lap. "We used to be such a close family," he said softly. "Then it all just fell apart. Every time I look at Skye, I see Mary . . ." Mr. Collinsworth's voice trailed off.

I swallowed the lump in my throat two, three, four times.

Mr. Collinsworth stood from his chair and squared his shoulders. "Well, then." He cleared his throat. "Say hello to your father for me, won't you?"

I nodded, my hand on the doorknob. I felt I should say something else before I ran out of there. "When you see Skye, tell her . . ." Tell her what? What would I say to Skye when I saw her again?

I didn't have to wonder long because when I opened the door she was standing right there.

* * * * *

"I told him everything, Skye," I blurted.

"All about the cheating and the lying and stealing. I'm sorry. I had to."

She glared at me. "You had to? What do you mean, you had to?" I felt my face turn six shades of red.

"Skye, is that you? Come in here," Mr. Collinsworth said.

Skye shot me eye daggers. Under her breath she hissed, "I can't believe you did this. Some friend you are. I'm sorry I ever met you. I hate you, Kacie Shannon. I hate your guts!"

"No, Skye." Mr. Collinsworth stood in the doorway, shaking his head. "Kacie did the right thing by coming to me. I see now how terribly I've been neglecting you. I've been so immersed in this election, so busy with my own life, my own needs . . ." He shook his head. "I'm sorry." They locked eyes.

"Oh, Daddy." Skye ran into his arms.

I had to get out of there or I was going to lose it. I fled for the bus stop. As I took a seat on the bench to wait, I closed my eyes and repeated over and over to myself, *It doesn't matter. It's all over now. You did what you had to do. It doesn't matter what she says anymore. It doesn't matter.*

But it did. She said she hated my guts. No one had ever said that to me before.

As soon as I got off the bus, I burst into tears and raced for home. All I wanted was to curl up in bed, put on my headphones, and tune out the world for the rest of my life.

But it wasn't to be. When I opened the door at home, Vicky was there, waiting at the bottom of the stairs.

"Kacie, hi. Your mom let me in and—" Her smile vanished. "What's wrong?"

"Oh, Vicky." I sank down onto the steps and covered my face with my hands. The tears just gushed.

"What is it, Kace?" Vicky asked gently. She put an arm around my shoulder. "What's going on? Come on, talk to me."

The words I had wanted to hear for so long. Now I couldn't form one intelligible word.

"Kace," Vicky said, "I'm sorry I've been so busy lately. I know you're mad at me, and you have every right to be."

"Mad at you? You're the one who should be mad," I hiccuped. "I've been so stupid. Yeah, I needed to talk to you, but I could have waited instead of just jumping into

135

another friendship, like being best friends with you is so casual."

"Are you talking about Skye Collinsworth?"

I sniffled. "How did you know?"

"I tried to call you a few times, but it seemed as if you were always with her. I guess I was a little hurt—okay, jealous, too. I mean, we've always been like attached at the hip, you know? We've never had other really close friends. Well, there's Rob, but nerds don't count." She nudged me.

"Oh, Vicky. You wouldn't believe the mess I'm in with Rob."

She rested her head on my shoulder. "Yeah, I would. I talked to him this morning. And Kyle, too."

I groaned.

"But everything's okay. Kyle and I are going out this weekend."

"You are? That's a relief," I snuffled. "At least I didn't totally wreck your life."

"You could never do that. It's your life I'm worried about." Vicky made me look at her, eye to eye. "Now, tell me everything. I want to hear it all."

Everything I had been holding in

exploded in an avalanche of words. I told her about Skye and cheating on the tests, and the gifts and lies and all my mixed-up feelings. I told her about my meeting with Mr. Collinsworth today, and the confrontation with Skye.

"She said I went behind her back, Vicky. She said she's sorry we ever met. And . . . and she said she *hates* me." I felt the tears welling up again.

"Kace, she's got serious emotional problems. That girl needs professional help. You were a terrific friend to her, and I think you actually did her a favor by telling her father. Maybe now they'll both get some help."

A tear rolled off my cheek. "You really think so?"

She nodded. "I really do."

I inhaled a shaky breath. "I still don't want her to hate me," I said. "Even after everything that's happened, I don't hate her."

Vicky said, "I don't think she does hate you, Kace. Not really. She was just lashing out."

I sighed. Vicky was probably right. But if

that were true . . . "Maybe after a while, after Skye and her father work things out, maybe I'll give her a call. I still think she needs a friend."

Vicky tilted her head toward me. "See what I mean? You're the greatest friend a person could ever have."

"What's going to happen between *us*, Vicky? Everything's different this year. You have so many things in your life now that don't include me."

She started to protest, but I stopped her. "It's okay, if that's what makes you happy. But I still want us to be friends—which doesn't mean we have to do everything together all the time. I can do some things by myself. In fact, I can do some things pretty well by myself."

"Really?" She smiled. "Like what?"

"Well, incredible as it may seem, I'm not half-bad at algebra."

She laughed. "I told you that you were good at math. In fact, you're good at a lot of things. If you'd just believe in yourself, you could do anything you wanted."

"Geez, you sound like this best friend

I used to have."

"Still have." She kicked my foot. "I hope. I really am sorry about not being there for you, Kace. I sort of overdosed on activities this year. I joined too many clubs and committees, plus going out, and cheerleading, and trying to study. I'm like totally stressed out. I'm dropping half that stuff."

"You don't have to on my account."

"I know."

We didn't speak for a minute. Then Vicky looked at me, blinking back tears. "Oh, Kace. I didn't mean to lock you out. I didn't even realize it was happening. Even with everything I was involved in, I knew there was something missing from my life. You! Our friendship. There hasn't been anyone to share with."

She paused, then added, "I'm so scared of losing you."

I put my arm around her. "No chance. Who else could possibly understand the importance of 'Voulez-vous laver mes chaussettes?'"

Vicky burst into laughter.

"Oh, by the way," she said, "I put the

Harrelson money in our Paris account. And I forgot to mention that when Kyle asked me out, he wanted to know if you'd be interested in coming along."

"As chaperone? Forget it."

She pressed her shoulder into mine. "No, silly. As his best friend's date. I guess there's this guy who's been dying to meet you."

"You're kidding. Someone's dying to meet me? And you forgot to mention it?" I grabbed her around the neck and started to shake.

"Actually," she coughed, removing my hands and holding them, "I was saving it as a surprise."

"Geez, Vicky. Some surprise. I don't know if I want my first date to be a blind date. What if he takes one look at me and—"

"Who said it was a blind date? You know him."

"I do?"

She pursed her lips. "If I remember correctly, you used to mention him once or twice." She paused for dramatic effect, until she saw my fist heading her way. Quickly, she added, "It's Daniel Oakes!"

Just as I started to shriek, the doorbell rang.

"I'll get it," Vicky said, jumping up to leave me in shock, with my mouth hanging open.

When I looked up, Rob was standing there, his brow furrowed. "Are you all right?" he asked.

"No, I'm not all right. I'm outstanding!" I leaped to my feet to give him a playful sock in the shoulder. Then I remembered he might still be mad at me. When he shadow-boxed back, though, I knew everything was all right.

"I just came from Tanya's," he said. "I can't believe this Skye person."

"It's a long story," I said, looking at Vicky. "But I take it things are okay between you and Tanya."

"Better than okay. Outstanding."

Vicky and I oohed, then laughed when Rob's face flushed beet red.

"Listen, Kacie," he mumbled, "I'm sorry. I was a little, well, perturbed and—"

"'Perturbed.' Did you hear that, Vicky? Rob was perturbed."

"Sounds painful."

Rob rolled his eyes. "Mad, okay? I was so mad! I said some things I didn't mean, and I jumped to some conclusions, and, well, I'm sorry."

I smiled at him. "I know, Rob. I'm sorry too."

"No hard feelings?"

"Of course not." Then I did punch him in the ribs.

He caught my wrist and held it. "In that case, I think there's a table waiting for us at the Dairy Kreme, and a Butterfinger Blitz with your name on it. My treat."

"No way," I said.

Vicky and Rob looked at me like I'd suffered permanent brain damage. She said, *"You're* refusing a Butterfinger Blitz?"

I linked one arm in Vicky's and the other in Rob's and, smiling from friend to friend, said, "Are you nuts? But this one's on me."

About the Author

Julie Anne Peters's love for reading began when she discovered teen romances—which she still enjoys reading. But many of her books and stories focus on friendship because, she says, "I believe friends are precious treasures to be cherished."

Her family moved to Colorado when she was five, and from her home, which she shares with a lot of cats, she can gaze out her window every morning at the Rocky Mountains and be instantly inspired.

Julie didn't start out as a writer. "I began my career teaching fifth grade," she explains, "but I was a terrible teacher. So I returned to college for a degree in computer science, then went on to get my MBA. In addition to teaching I've been employed as a secretary, research assistant, computer programmer, systems analyst, and concessionaire at the zoo."

When Julie isn't writing, she works part-time in an elementary school tutoring special-needs children. Her hobbies include reading, cross-stitching, traveling, walking, and cheering on the Denver Broncos.

Risky Friends is her first book for Willowisp Press.